THE RANCHER TAKES A COWGIRL

TEXAS RANCHER TRILOGY ~ BOOK 3

MISTY M. BELLER

Unless otherwise indicated, all Scripture quotations are taken from the Holy Bible, Kings James Version.

ISBN-13: 9780998208787

To my sweet angel Haven.
I love you more than you could ever imagine.

To give light to them that sit in darkness and in the shadow of death,
to guide our feet into the way of peace.

Luke 1:79 (KJV)

CHAPTER 1

April 10, 1876
Double Rocking B Ranch ~ Near Seguin, Texas

"Boss, you better come quick, but you're not gonna like it."

Monty Dominguez scanned the stable boy's pensive face as he reined Poncho to a halt. "Trouble?" His throat tightened as he swung to the ground.

"Not sure. I don't think so. Leastways not the kind yer thinkin'. Miz O'Brien needs ya in the big house."

As Monty turned toward the sprawling, two-story log home, his muscles stiffened. If Anna needed him, were she or the children in danger? Ill? Her husband, Jacob, had ridden the two hours to Seguin that afternoon for business, leaving care of his family with Monty, as the ranch foreman. If anything happened to them under his watch...

He extended his stride and took the five porch steps in two leaps. Not stopping to knock, he pushed through the door and tossed his hat on the wall peg. The O'Briens always had an open-door attitude toward the ranch hands, even feeding the entire crew meals from the dining room table. But had their way of thinking put them in danger today?

Voices drifted from the parlor, and Monty strode that direction, stopping in the doorway to let his eyes adjust to the dimness. Anna stood with the baby in her arms, speaking with another woman by the hearth.

Both pairs of eyes turned on him and the murmuring stopped.

"Monty." Anna flashed an eager smile as she shifted her infant son in her arms. Did she look relieved to see him?

Monty's gaze scanned the other woman. At least, she might be a woman. Yes, the curves outlined by her snug leather vest were plenty feminine, and her long brown braid added to that image. But the gun belt hanging from her hips, and the men's boots peering from beneath her leather chaps, gave a very different impression.

Was she wearing pants? A bit of brown cotton gathered around the edges of the chaps. If that was supposed to be a split skirt, she might as well have been wearing men's wool trousers.

"Monty?"

His gaze zipped back to Anna, who eyed him with both brows raised. He must have missed whatever she'd said. "Sorry. What?"

"I'd like you to meet Miss Harper. She's just arrived from California and is hiring on to be one of our cowpunchers. You said you're looking for two more, right?"

Monty's mind struggled to make sense of her statement. He wasn't always such a simpleton, but the words *Miss* and *cowpuncher* didn't usually apply to the same person. Surely Anna didn't mean this woman planned to herd cattle with his men.

He scuffed the wooden floor with a boot and flicked his gaze back to the unfamiliar woman. Her hair had a wild look to it, with stray wisps flying out from the braid, and a flat line around her crown like she'd recently been wearing a hat. A man's hat.

Not the frilly kind women pinned on these days. Her face held a tan, especially across her lower cheeks and that strong pointed chin. She obviously wasn't a stranger to the sun.

But his focus kept coming back to those blue eyes, clear enough to be seen all the way across the room. Although the glare emanating from them might have something to do with their visibility.

"Monty." Anna's voice had quieted, and held a bit of a warning this time. She expected him to speak, and the tone of her voice told him her patience was wearing out quickly.

"Ma'am." He nodded toward the newcomer, then turned his focus back to Anna. "Would you mind a private word, Mrs. O'Brien?" Anna and Jacob were quite casual with their workers, Jacob even punching cattle with the men at times. But Monty never had gotten use to the idea of calling them by their given names in front of strangers.

Anna shot Miss Harper an apologetic look. "Please make yourself at home, Grace. I'll just pour a cup of coffee for Monty and be right back." She motioned toward the settee, then turned a steely glare on Monty as she swept toward him. The impact of her anger was softened though, when the babe in her arms gurgled and waved at Monty as they passed. Little Martin was a cute niño. At three months old, he'd learned to smile and squeal, and put both to good use now that he saw "Uncle Monty."

He gave a nod to the stranger, who still stood by the hearth, straight as a corral post. Then Monty turned on his heel and followed in Anna's icy wake toward the kitchen.

When they'd both entered the room in the rear of the house, Anna pushed the door shut behind them and spun to face him with a swish of skirts. Her face had heated a bright pink, with darker splashes covering her cheeks. And those brown eyes sparked fire. "What's wrong with you?"

How had the presence of that strange woman turned his boss's placid wife so temperamental? He could count on one hand the times he'd seen Anna lose her temper. Even when she'd first hired on to the ranch as cook seven years ago, before she married Jacob O'Brien and become doña of the place.

He dipped his head, showing respect but also picking through his thoughts to find the right words. "I'm still tryin' to figure the situation. What exactly are you askin' me to do with that woman?"

"Use her as one of your cow hands, Monty. Didn't you hear me in there?"

He scanned her face, he even tilted his head a bit to see if the angle helped. Cause there was obviously something here he wasn't seeing. "A woman? Working cattle?"

She let out a breath. "She's had a hard background. I don't know all the specifics, but she says she's been working cattle for more than nine years now. I think she can do the job, Monty, I do. Give her a chance."

She was really serious about this. Monty swallowed. How was he going to have a woman out working with the rest of the men? They knew how to bide their manners around the house, but out in the pastures they were pretty much rough-necks. That would have to end though, if this woman came on board. And where would she sleep? Certainly not in the bunkhouse with the boys.

"She can have a bedroom in the house here." Anna must have read his mind. "Or… I know." The babe started to fuss and she raised him to her shoulder. "What about the old bunkhouse?"

He pinched his mouth. "It leaks. Haven't been able to spare men for the repairs yet. Besides, I need it when we hire extra help next month."

Anna shrugged. "She can stay in the house then."

Nothing about this situation felt right. He was being forced to hire a woman as one of his cow hands. Who ever heard of such a thing? What had that lady done to convince Anna so thoroughly? And the mere fact that Anna would consider doing the hiring... Not even Jacob tried to usurp Monty's decisions about who did and didn't work with the cattle. That was the job of the ranch foreman, after all.

Letting out a long breath, he scrubbed a hand through his hair. "When do you want her to start?"

A ray of sunshine lit Anna's face. "We'll let her get settled in today, then she can begin work in the morning."

Monty nodded as he turned away. If he had to say yes now, so be it. But when Jacob came home, surely he could talk some sense into his wife.

~

Monty eased into his chair at the dinner table that night along with the rest of the boys. It still didn't feel right, sitting at the end of the table, where Jacob's pa had always reigned. But when the older man passed away three years ago, Jacob insisted Monty take the seat, while Jacob still sat at the other end of the oversize table.

A chair that was empty at the moment. The man had made it back from town, but the rumble of voices from the kitchen must mean he was helping Anna settle the children.

The rest of the boys were here though, along with the new female Anna hired, filling the empty chair between Santiago and Jesse. What was her name? Miss Harper, or something like that. The cow hands were eyeing her curiously, so Monty would have to introduce her soon. What a bunch of flack he'd get for hiring the woman. Maybe they'd at least hold their tongues until they were out of the big house.

He could hope.

Jacob stepped from the kitchen, followed by Mama Sarita, the ranch cook and housekeeper. He took his place at the far end of the table while the older woman settled a heaping plate of tortillas in an empty spot on the pecan wood surface. A savory aroma wafted from three oversize pots of Shepherd's pie, sending his stomach into a hungry knot.

Mama Sarita scuttled back toward the kitchen, and Jacob quickly scanned the faces around the table, his gaze ending on the new woman. "Anna's with the children, so I reckon' we'll say grace."

Jacob kept the prayer succinct and heartfelt, as usual. With his "Amen," the boys dove into the food, elbows flying as they loaded plates and started stuffing their gizzards.

Monty couldn't help but watch Miss Harper for her reaction to the scene. His boys worked hard, and mealtime was the favorite part of most days. They tended to be a bit overeager until their stomachs filled some. The sight had scared off more than one visitor from town, although Jacob and Anna insisted that the whole crew continue eating with the family.

Miss Harper's eyes didn't widen as he'd expected. They narrowed, taking in the lay of the land. Then with a quick hand, she snagged a tortilla from the serving plate as Santiago scooped it off the table.

The cow hand paused, his brows lifting as though he'd forgotten the strange woman beside him. Then a touch of red crept up his sun-roughened neck. "Sorry, ma'am." He held out the plate like a gift, and she nodded as she took a second tortilla. Santiago then reached out and scooped up the serving spoon from the nearest pot of shepherd's pie, and offered it to Miss Harper.

Her face softened and a corner of her mouth tipped toward the rough cowpoke. The first hint of a smile Monty had seen from her. Much nicer than the ridiculous grin that spread over Santiago's dark features.

Something hard struck Monty's leg under the table. He turned to eye Donato, one of his cousins and a longstanding hand on the Double Rocking B. Donato was just a few years older than Monty, and now raised an eyebrow at him. Monty returned the expression, and Donato gave a little jerk of his head down the table toward Miss Harper.

Monty let out a breath, his shoulders drooping as the air left him. Yes, it was time he made introductions. Before the men turned stupid around her. They obviously didn't see enough females during their days herding cattle. Well, that was about to change. But he'd be drawn and quartered before he let any sparkin' happen on his payroll.

He cleared his throat. Aside from the clatter of forks, the room quieted as sixteen pairs of eyes turned toward him. Including Jacob's. "Reckon' ya'll should meet the new cowhand." He nodded toward the woman. "Miss Harper joined on today. She'll be ridin' out with us tomorrow."

Every bit of noise in the room ceased, and several jaws dropped. Manuel crossed himself and mumbled something under his breath. Jacob was the first to move again, as he scooped up a fork full of mashed potatoes and dipped his chin to eat it. He didn't meet Monty's gaze, just focused on his food.

What did he think about his wife's new hire? Surely she'd told him before dinner, because he hadn't seemed surprised to see the woman at the table. But his lack of communication now spoke volumes. After the meal was over, Monty would pin the man down and get some answers. There were too many things he wasn't being told about Miss Harper.

Donato was the first to speak as he looked down the table and nodded toward the lady. "Welcome, ma'am." Good ol' Donato. The man had long been his right hand on the ranch. And a good friend besides.

The others responded in kind, and Miss Harper offered a few nods and a "Nice to meet you all."

And that was about the last word spoken during the meal. As soon as the plates were scraped clean, the men stood and excused themselves.

Within minutes, the only people left in the room with him

were Jacob and Miss Harper. Monty pushed from the table and stood.

"Mr. Dominguez, do you have any instructions for me?" The voice was very female, but strong. Like it could carry across a herd of lowing cattle.

Monty turned to face the woman. "Be ready to ride out after breakfast. You'll be assigned horses then."

"All right." She stood there another minute, her blue eyes watching him. Her braid lay over her shoulder, but neater now than it had been earlier. But why was he noticing that kind of thing?

He pulled his gaze from the woman to his boss, who stood and pushed in his chair. "Jacob, do you have a minute?"

A smile tugged at Jacob's mouth. "I do. You want coffee in the office?"

Monty nodded. Jacob must know what was coming since he picked the most private room in the house.

A motion pulled at the corner of his gaze, but Monty forced his eyes not to track Miss Harper's progress as she strode past him and out the door.

CHAPTER 2

"I have to know what's going on, Jacob. This doesn't feel right." Monty stared out the window into the darkness, watching the flicker of lantern light in the barn outside. Juan must still be settling in the horses for the night. Or Chester, the stable boy, milking the cow.

Monty turned back to face Jacob, who relaxed in one of the two upholstered chairs along the empty library wall. This man had been like a brother to him, ever since Monty showed up at the O'Brien ranch at twelve years old, orphaned and hungry. Jacob's Pa had been Monty's in every way that mattered, teaching them both how to raise cattle and care for the land.

He couldn't imagine a better life than the one he lived now, here on the Double Rocking B, working alongside his best friend. Most days, anyway.

It was nice to see Jacob settled and happy. Anna was perfect for him. Not that the rest of the hands hadn't taken a strong liking to her in the beginning, Monty chief among them. But it'd been clear from the start she had eyes for no one but Jacob. The battle was over before the rest of them had half a chance.

But that seemed to be the way of things when it came to him

and women. Every time a possible prospect came along, she was snapped up before he could gather his breath to say howdy.

Jacob shrugged, but met Monty's eye squarely. "I really don't know, Monty."

Monty had to blink to pull himself back to the conversation.

His friend kept talking, though. "Anna said the lady needs a job. Came from a tough situation in California."

A growl found its way up Monty's throat. "What tough situation? The kind with trouble that'll follow her here?" If she brought danger to the O'Brien family, he'd personally make her pay.

Jacob's brows pulled together. "I doubt anything would follow her a thousand miles from California to Texas. It didn't sound like she was in trouble with the law. Anna wouldn't have hired her if that were the case." He sighed and sank back in the chair, cradling his coffee mug with both hands. "I'm sorry Anna stepped on your toes by doing the hiring. I trust her instincts, though. If she thought Miss Harper would be good here, don't you think we could give her a try?"

What could Monty say to that? He scrubbed a hand through his hair and turned back to the window. "I guess."

Looked like he didn't have a choice. He'd definitely keep an eye on the woman. And if there was any inkling her secrets would put the O'Brien family or the ranch in danger, she'd be out like a squirrel ahead of a pack of hungry coyote.

~

Grace stared at herself in the mirror over the dressing table in the early morning light, trying to see her reflection the way the others would. Her bandana was the same as the men wore. Her vest, too, although she'd had to take it up considerably to fit snug enough so it didn't interfere when she swung a lariat. She'd not seen the other men wearing gun belts, but she wasn't about to be caught without her Colt single action army revolver. There was too much chance *he'd* followed her.

She tucked a strand of dark brown hair back in her braid, then picked up her hat from the table's surface. Mr. Dominguez had seemed none too pleased to add her to the payroll yesterday. But surely when he saw how she could work right alongside the men, he'd settle in to the idea.

He wasn't what she'd expected either, though. Those brooding eyes and dark features. And young. Well, maybe not young. But not half as old as Rusty, the foreman on Papa's ranch for as far back as she could remember.

Grace swallowed down a burn in her throat. She wouldn't be working with Rusty anymore. Not ever. So she'd best buckle down and win over the new boss. Gripping her hat brim, she pulled open the bedroom door.

Breakfast was another quiet affair, just like dinner had been the night before. The men seemed uneasy. Because of her? Or because they were all piled into the fancy dining room in the big house? She'd never seen a ranch where the hired help ate with the family. Back in California, theirs and every other ranch around fed the cow hands under a lean-to off the cook house.

She paced herself to finish at the same time as the men on either side of her. One had given his name as Santiago, but she didn't catch the other's. When they all stood and filed toward the door, Grace did the same.

"Santiago."

When the man in front of her stopped in his tracks, Grace barely caught herself before smacking into him.

"Sí, boss." Santiago eyed Mr. Dominguez.

"You're in charge of Miss Harper today. Tell Juan to give her one of those three-year-olds he's finished with. I want you two with the main herd while the rest of us ride the outside lines."

Grace fought the urge to nibble her lip. Might as well speak up now instead of waiting. She took a step to the side so she could see both men. "Call me Grace."

Both heads swiveled to face her, along with everyone else in hearing distance. What was wrong with these men that they froze every time she spoke up? Hadn't they seen a woman before?

She raised her chin and met Mr. Dominguez's gaze.

He raised a single brow. "All right. Santiago, you and *Grace* stay with the herd." Then he turned and strode from the room.

Juan, the aging wrangler in the barn, brought Grace what seemed like a decent mare. A bit leggy still, but the muscle along her shoulders and haunches was well-defined, and her chest would continue to widen with regular work.

"You think we'll get along, girl?" Grace kept up a steady murmur as she settled her saddle blanket on the chestnut mare and reached for the saddle. The horse stood quiet, only shifting a foot to balance her weight as Grace settled the heavy leather on her back.

"I call this one Pepper, because her coat in the spring is as red as a habanero." Juan approached the mare's off side and rested a hand on her shoulder. "She'll be good for you. Is still learning to think like the cattle, but she has a nice gait that won't be hard to sit a long day." The man's heavy Mexican accent laced each word, and his wrinkled smile gave him a gentle look. Like he would be most comfortable gathering the children on his knees to tell stories.

"I'm sure we'll get along fine." Grace pulled the cinch tight and stroked the mare's neck. She could imagine the fire of the chestnut hairs once the mare shed the thick, wooly winter coat. "The mare I came with should be fine for me to ride again after she's had a few days' rest. Georgina's a good cow horse, but it was a long trip from California. She deserves a break."

"Sí."

Several figures came into view through the barn door. The

men were ready to ride out. Grabbing her bridle, Grace slipped it over the mare's head, then placed her left boot into the stirrup and vaulted into the seat. Home. She settled into the comfort of the leather as it encased her legs. No matter where she was, the back of a horse had been home for as long as she could remember.

Giving the old wrangler a thankful smile, she signaled the mare forward and headed toward the rest of the group.

Santiago reined over to her with a grin, and Pepper fell into step with his bay gelding. As they rode, the man shared bits and pieces about the ranch. His voice held a hint of Mexican accent, but not nearly as strong as Juan's. In fact, over half the men now riding out toward the pastures shared the same dark coloring of Mexican vaqueros. Not an unusual sight for Grace, since most of the cow hands on their ranch in California had at one time come over the border from Mexico.

Her gaze wandered up to Mr. Dominguez. He rode tall and comfortable on a paint gelding, one hand gripping his reins and the other resting easily on his chap-covered leg. He certainly could sit a horse—and look good doing it.

The man riding beside him spoke, and Mr. Dominguez glanced at him with a word and a smile. The look softened his face in a way she'd not seen on him before, certainly not when he looked at *her*.

Something tugged in her chest. She'd have to make an effort to get one of those smiles from him.

Soon, they topped a hill and a wide valley spread out before them, surrounded by trees on two sides, and open land on the other two. A massive herd of longhorns grazed across the area. Grace inhaled a deep, cleansing breath. The familiar aroma of dust and manure and cow hide all blended together, easing a bit of tension from her shoulders.

The men fanned out, scattering in pairs around the outskirts of the herd. Santiago motioned for her to follow him toward the tree line along the western side.

"The others will be searching for the wanderers, but we're to keep the animals close to the herd. Next week, after all the cattle are gathered, we'll do the branding. Then comes the big roundup with the other ranches."

Grace nodded. "How many ranches are in the area?"

Santiago shrugged, his dark eyes widening. "I don't know—fifteen, twenty. But not many as big as the Double Rocking B. Señor Jacob and his Pa, they are good with the cattle and good with the men. Monty, too, although don't tell my cousin I say good things about him." He gave her a wink.

Mr. Dominguez was his cousin? To be expected, she supposed. Perhaps that's why the foreman had assigned Santiago to work with her. Someone to determine whether she was up to the job. Maybe once Santiago saw her capabilities, the grim boss would relax his concerns.

"How far does the ranch property spread?" They were entering the woods now, so Grace reined her mare back behind Santiago's horse.

"It follows the Guadalupe River along the south side. Prettiest sight on the property, too. Then two-fork creek on the west. We call this the north pasture, and it's where we'll do the branding, and where we keep 'em in the worst of the winter. There's a line shack down in that far corner if the weather turns bad." He motioned toward the northeast. "Then there's another little pasture on the other side of the house. All told, I think it's close to five hundred acres or so. Jacob's bought up a couple of small ranches since his pa died."

Grace gulped, but tried not to look too surprised. In California, their three-hundred-twenty-acre ranch had been one of the largest in the area, which meant Pa was one of the wealthiest and most influential men within three counties. This Jacob O'Brien seemed awfully young to hold that same standing.

A low mournful sound drifted through the trees ahead of them, and Grace followed Santiago as he turned that direction. "Looks like a little one's got himself stuck."

The calf came into view as they rode closer, tangled in a hopeless mess of vines and briars. They'd not had such thick underbrush in California. Mostly cactus and sagebrush.

Santiago dismounted and pulled a long knife from a scabbard on his saddle. Grace slid to the ground and wove her way through the vines until she stood a few feet from the animal's head.

The calf looked to be a yearling, or maybe a little younger, with pointy horns about six inches long. But those six inches stuck straight out, and were now wrapped snuggly in the vines and underbrush. The animal stood with its head locked tight, neck contorted in an obviously uncomfortable position. Poor fellow.

She glanced back at Santiago, who was trying to cut his way through a cluster of vines to get close enough. "Here. I can get most of the vines from where I'm standing." Grace held out her hand for the knife.

He hesitated, taking in her position compared to his own. He looked about to speak, then clamped his mouth shut and extended the knife to her—handle first—through a gap in the brush.

Grace pinched her lips against a smile. It would take time for them to trust her, but at least this man was willing to try.

She crooned to the young bull while she sliced away his restraints, and the animal stood mostly still. But as his bonds loosened, the calf grew restless, pulling and jerking to free himself.

"When he's free, we should mount quickly." Santiago eyed the squirming creature. "If the animals are tangled for long, they become nasty. Were he much bigger, I would not have left my horse's back."

Grace glanced back to flash the man a wry smile. Yes, she was familiar with a longhorn's temper.

When only a single, thin vine held the animal, she backed out of the brush. As the calf thrashed to clear himself from his entrapments, she and Santiago sprinted toward their horses and mounted.

One of the first things Rusty had taught her on Papa's ranch was respect for the longhorns. Of course, the teaching hadn't really sunk in until she'd experienced the dangers firsthand, when she'd dismounted to free a young calf trapped between two rocks. The mother cow hadn't appreciated her efforts as much as Grace would have expected. It was a wonder she'd walked away with only a scar on her thigh to remember the experience. That incident had also given her a healthy respect for a well-made pair of leather chaparejos, even in the scorching southern California sun. She hadn't worked cattle without them, since that day nine years ago.

Of course, that danger was nothing compared to what she was running from now.

~

Monty watched from the edge of the tree line as Grace and her horse emerged from the far patch of woods, herding three steers toward the larger herd. He'd stayed close most of the day, just out of sight to keep an eye on her. But she seemed to handle herself well with the animals. He'd expected Santiago to keep her at his side all day, just in case she made any green mistakes that might endanger her or the horse. But the man had allowed her to work alone for several hours now, checking in every so often. Had she already sweet-talked his cousin into ignoring his better judgment? Maybe it wasn't such a good idea to let her team up with Santiago this first day.

Monty had always kept the new riders at his own side until he was sure they had enough cow sense not to get hurt. But something about this woman put him off-balance, and it had seemed like a good idea to keep a bit of distance. Was it only the danger that concerned him? She'd certainly seemed like bad news from the start, and what little Jacob had told him last evening was enough for Monty to stew in his thoughts all night.

Lord, show me what to do with this woman.

The idea for her to shadow Santiago had seemed like a good compromise. Monty could keep an eye on her from a distance, without having to spend time in her company. And Santiago seemed smitten enough to ensure the woman's safety.

A niggle of shame crept up Monty's chest. It wasn't right of him to take advantage of one of his men that way. He'd always said he'd never ask any of the hands to do something he wouldn't do himself. But that's just what he'd done.

Tomorrow, would be different.

Monty nudged Poncho forward and rode into the meadow. Maybe time with her tomorrow would help him get a better read on the woman's intentions.

And the danger she brought with her.

CHAPTER 3

The next morning, Grace found herself riding beside her tall boss, heading a different direction than the rest of the cowpunchers. He'd said he wanted to show her the lay of the land today, although she suspected it had more to do with keeping an eye on her. She'd caught glimpses of him yesterday, watching from the trees, or just over the slope of the hill.

It seemed today his observation would be a bit more blatant. Did he really think she was so inept she had to be supervised like a nursemaid with a child? But maybe this would be an opportunity. He could see her interact with the animals, and perhaps she could get him talking—break through whatever barrier stood between them.

She inhaled a breath, cutting a glance at his stoic form. Now was as good a time as any to start. "Have you worked on this ranch long, Mr. Dominguez?"

He didn't look at her, didn't show any visible reaction to her words. In fact, for several moments, Grace wasn't sure he'd even heard them. Did the man have a bad ear?

"Been here since I was twelve."

Twelve. She slid another sideways glance toward him. The man looked to be five or six years older than her, which would put him in his early thirties. So he'd worked at this ranch for twenty years? That was loyalty in its purest form. No wonder he sat a horse and rode this land like he belonged here.

"That's impressive." She wanted to ask more, but every question she could think of sounded like prying. Had his parents died young? For surely they wouldn't let their twelve-year-old leave home to work full-time on a ranch.

"You've hired on as a cowhand before?"

The question pulled her from her thoughts. The man spoke without being prompted? A wonder. "I worked on my father's ranch in California. Not such a big spread as you have here, but a decent size." And that was all she planned to say on the place. Any more would give away too many details. Make it too easy to connect a stranger's questions to her.

"You punched cattle there?"

"For the last nine years. Growing up, he always kept me with him out on the range—when Mama would let him. But after she died, there was nothing to stop me."

"I'm surprised your father allowed you to leave. I wouldn't easily part with a good cow hand."

She almost missed the tilt of his chin as he stole a glance at her. But the insinuation was clear. "My father didn't have a choice in the matter. He died six months ago." And that was *all* she would say about her family, even if she had to be rude to keep silent.

He didn't probe farther though, and the tension in her neck gradually eased under the steady rhythm of her mare's stride. Yet, the strain thickened the air between them. What could she say to put him at ease? She'd have to prove herself, she knew. But it would be much easier if they could start off on level ground. Or at least a gentle slope, not a rocky cliff.

Summoning her courage and a deep breath, she started in. "Mr. Dominguez—"

"Monty."

She blinked at the lightning-quick interruption. "All right. Monty." The name fit him. Strong, rugged. Very masculine. She swallowed to gather her thoughts again. "I'm sorry if we got off on the wrong foot that first day. I'd like to make a clean start if we can."

He didn't even try to hide the look he sent her way. Appraising. But she couldn't decipher the result of his assessment. Did he think her too bold? Surely not. Men out west appreciated honesty. At least, men of her acquaintance in California had. The decent ones, that is.

"Not sure you'd wanna go all the way back to the start."

Was that a touch of humor in his voice? Sarcastic humor maybe. Was he implying she wouldn't have the job if they started over? Grace sat a bit straighter. "You mean you wouldn't have hired me?" She'd known she might have a challenge finding work in a man's occupation, but from her first conversation with Mrs. O'Brien, it seemed the folks at this ranch wouldn't be as prejudice against her gender. Maybe she'd been wrong.

"Not sayin' that. Just that I wasn't given the choice." He drawled the words, but the slow cadence only gave them more punch.

Grace sucked in a breath as the bigger picture came clear before her. When Mrs. O'Brien had seemed to force him to accept her choice to hire Grace, it wasn't because he'd disliked employing a woman. It was because *he* was the one who usually handled the hiring.

Hadn't Mrs. O'Brien said during their initial interview that she'd never hired a cow hand before? Grace had assumed that meant her husband usually handled such matters. But when she'd offered to wait for the man, Mrs. O'Brien had waved the concern away. Back home, either Papa or Rusty hired on help, depending on who the prospective employee spoke with first. But that must not be the case on this ranch. Not with this man, who wore his authority like a well-broken-in hat.

She had to clear up the matter, and maybe an apology would help. "I'm sorry if you felt ramrodded into hiring me, sir. That wasn't my intent. I merely asked to speak with the boss of the place and was escorted to Mrs. O'Brien. I offered to wait for her husband to discuss employment, but she said it wasn't necessary. Back home, either my father or our foreman handled hiring matters. But I realize that's not the case everywhere. My apologies if I overstepped. That wasn't my intent."

The outline of his solid posture didn't change as she spoke, nor in the long minutes of silence afterward, but a furrow formed in his brow. She knew that look well, although she was used to seeing it on a much older face. Rusty's lines would crease into deep grooves when he was mulling over his response to a situation.

She typically gave Rusty time to think, but maybe one more tidbit would help this man come to a positive conclusion. "I just want you to know, sir, I'll work hard for you. I have good experience with cattle, and you won't be sorry to have me on your payroll."

The corner of his mouth twitched, and after several beats, he offered only a single nod.

She'd take it. Grace settled back in the saddle and eased out a breath. Maybe the explanation had helped. At least she'd done what she could.

Now it was time to show what she was made of. She could only hope it would be enough.

~

Grace rubbed the itchy spot behind Georgina's ears, as the calming effect of the evening darkness settled over the barnyard. A horse snorted in the distance, answered by the chirrup of a cricket and the stomp of an animal's hoof. A ranch after dark could be a magical thing, whether in California or Texas.

The mare bobbed her head, pressing into Grace's hand, protesting the fact that her scratching had slowed. "You like that, girl?"

A soft thud sounded from inside the bunkhouse, where a glimmer of light shone under the door. The men had settled in quietly after caring for their equipment following dinner. She should be doing the same.

But after an entire day under Monty's shadow, she'd needed a few quiet moments with her old sidekick. Just her and the animals. Not that Monty had been rude or hard to work with. In fact, they hadn't really done much work. Mostly rode from one pasture to the next, checking stock and cowboys. He showed her the property boundaries on each side, and they followed the Guadalupe River for a long stretch. Santiago had been right about its beauty. The gentle flowing sound of the clear water soaked into her soul, settling peace over her—if only for a moment. Monty had even given her a chance to dismount and touch the frigid river water.

None of his actions today had been rude. But something sparked between them, building the tension as the day progressed. Not something she could quite put a finger on. Maybe...awareness? After the first hour or so, his companionship hadn't felt awkward. Yet she'd been painfully conscious of every movement he made. Every glance her way. The few times their eyes had met...

She'd jerked away from each look. But that wasn't her style at all. She usually met confrontation head on, with a measured scrutiny. Until she had a good grasp on what she was up against, and a good idea of how she'd handle it.

And then there was the matter of church tomorrow. Monty made it clear she'd be expected to attend, along with the rest of the cowhands. She had nothing against going to the service. She'd rarely missed a Sunday at home in the little chapel on the ranch, especially when Mama was alive.

But could she really chance meeting that many people? Monty had said they attended the larger of the two churches in town. Not many people forgot the presence of a female cowhand. So many people who might remember her, if a stranger showed up asking about a new woman in town.

A sigh leaked out. She'd hoped her chosen occupation could help her hide. Leonard surely wouldn't suspect she'd take up cowpunching on a stranger's ranch. But this career might be a double-edged sword.

But in for a penny, in for a pound. She'd committed to it, so she'd have to make the best of things. Stay on her toes. And away from people.

So what about church? Maybe if she appealed to Anna, the woman could speak with Monty on her behalf. Anna seemed to understand Grace's fears that first day, even without knowing the details.

But no. She wouldn't go around Monty again. The man was her boss, after all. She'd have to follow his orders whether she liked it or not. And who knew, maybe he'd be lenient. But how to explain her reasons without actually giving them away?

As if summoned by her thoughts, the front door on the main house opened, and the profile of a man's broad shoulders darkened the light spilling onto the porch. She'd been watching those same shoulders most of the day, admiring the way his well-defined muscles played under his shirt. Now only a dark outline in the doorway, the breadth of him scorched the moisture from her mouth.

Grace swallowed. Her heart had picked up its pace, but she had no reason to be nervous around him. And here was the perfect time to discuss tomorrow morning's church service.

She gave Georgina a final pat, then stepped away from the corral fence to meet Monty on the path to the bunkhouse.

He caught her movement without any obvious surprise. Had he known she was there? Or did nothing ruffle this man? Everything about him exuded sturdiness. Just like Rusty had. Must go with the job of foreman. Yet, this man had an extra strength, more than anyone else she'd known.

He stopped about five steps in front of her, the moon to his back so she couldn't see more than shadows on his face. But that meant he could see her clearly.

Silence reigned as she searched for the right words.

"Nice night." His voice was quiet, and the words not at all what she'd expected.

"Yes." Grace's hands came up to rub her arms. "A bit cooler than California."

A low chuckle rumbled from him. "This is a warm spell for us. But I hope it will last."

A warm spell. Of course. She swallowed. "Monty, I have a question. A favor, really."

His only response was a slight nod. Although maybe the movement was only him settling in to hear her request.

"You mentioned church tomorrow. I wondered if I could have permission to stay here instead? I prefer to read Scripture on my own." Well, that wasn't completely a lie. She would prefer to stay at the ranch and read Scripture over being seen by all those people. Grace didn't dare breathe as she watched him for an answer.

Monty's head tipped a bit. "The Scripture says not to forsake the assembling of the saints."

"I know. It's just…" She fumbled for something that might make sense, but no better words found her tongue. "I would prefer to stay here tomorrow, if I might have your permission." She fought to keep from dropping her chin, like a child awaiting punishment for sneaking candy.

Monty was silent for several interminable moments. Grace's heartbeat pulsed loud in her ears. Could he hear it?

"If it's that important, I suppose you can do your own studies tomorrow. I'd prefer you attend with the rest of us in the future, though."

Grace exhaled, strength leaking from her bones with the spent air. "Thank you." She'd been given at least one week's reprieve. But would that really help?

He watched her for another moment, and the skin along Grace's arms prickled. What was he searching for? It was as if his dark eyes pierced through her skin to her very thoughts.

She forced her chin up. "I suppose I should head inside now. Thanks again."

He nodded, and she stepped forward, taking a wide berth around him.

"G'night."

The word drifted to her after she'd already passed him, sending a rush of bumps skittering over her shoulders. What was it about this man that brought on her body's strange responses?

As Grace let herself into the main house, the high pitch of a little girl's voice drifted from the parlor, along with the low rumble of a man's tones. She stopped in the doorway. Did she dare ask another special request?

"Grace." Anna sounded pleased to see her, as she snuggled the baby in a rocker by the fire. Her husband and older daughter nestled in the overstuffed chair beside her. "Won't you come sit with us?"

Grace tried to summon a thankful smile. "No, thank you. I'll just head on up for the night. Although..." She paused to gather the right words. "I wonder if it would bother you if I played the violin for a few minutes before retiring?"

"Oh, really?" Anna's face lit. "I had no idea you played an instrument. Yes, please. We'd love it." Pure delight rang through the words.

Grace nodded. "Thank you. I'll keep my door closed so the noise doesn't bother you." Although, to play the way she craved, the sound would ring through the entire house. But that couldn't happen tonight. She was only a hired hand, and the last thing she wanted to do was disturb the family. How different from her life six months ago.

As she latched the door of her private quarters, Grace's gaze fell on the leather violin case she'd tucked in the corner. Her most treasured gift from Mama. The one thing they'd had in common. When there was nothing else they could agree on, the two of them could lay bow to string and find harmony. Breath-taking, heart-stirring harmony.

Her fingers fumbled as she untied the leather clasps. When she raised the cover, her eyes roamed the polished wood inside. Perfect. She'd had the case tied so carefully in her bedroll, the long ride to Texas hadn't seemed to phase it.

After plucking the strings to find the perfect tuning, she lifted the violin to her shoulder and tucked it under her chin. Fitting her fingers around the bow, she closed her eyes, and allowed the music to soak in.

With the rich melody of Mendelsson's Violin Concerto filling her veins, Grace's mind cleared. If she could just hide out until Leonard stopped looking for her, maybe she could finally live a normal life in this place. Her new home.

~

Monty lay on his bed in the corner of the bunkhouse, soaking in the dissonant strains of music drifting through the walls. Was that Grace? It had to be. Such rich sounds had never flowed from the main house before.

Where had she ever learned to play an instrument that way? It was unlike anything he'd heard. Touching a place deep inside him.

That woman was such a mystery. Her speech sounded polished, not like any cow hand he'd ever met. Yet she didn't seemed compelled to prattle on like most females. She'd seemed to have decent knowledge about the animals, and a light came into her eyes when she spoke of the ranch she'd left in California. Her father's, apparently. Tough lot that both her parents had passed on. He certainly knew how that felt.

So what was she doing half a continent away, working as a hired hand? It made no sense. Why hadn't she married and stayed to run her own ranch? Or were there other siblings who'd inherited the property, so she struck out on her own? So many questions.

Now more than before, he wanted to learn her secrets. Wanted to know the many facets of Grace Harper. Intriguing.

CHAPTER 4

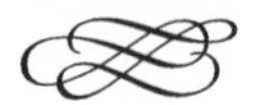

Monty eased Poncho forward to loosen the rope around the calf as Donato took control of the feisty heifer. The animal let out another pitiful bleat as the man tied its feet and slipped the lariat off her neck. If the little thing thought being caught was bad, she'd not enjoy what was coming next. It had to be done though, and the pain from branding would soon fade, leaving the security that she'd stay in the lush pastures of the Double Rocking B.

As he gathered the loops of his rope, Monty scanned each of the stations. After Donato and Nathan branded each animal, Jesse stepped forward to notch the calf's ear with the Double Rocking B's special marking. Just in case the brand was ever disfigured. Then the young bulls moved on to the next station to be castrated. It looked like Carlos, Luis, and—his gaze froze at the smaller figure hunched over the back end of a prostrate male calf.

Grace? The glint of a metal blade shimmered in the sun, and Monty nudged his horse closer as his throat tightened. Surely they hadn't forced Grace to rotate into the worst of the stations. Last time he'd seen her, she'd had a branding iron in her hand, which was bad enough. How could these roughnecks make a woman take on such a bloody, distasteful job?

When he was a few strides away, Monty slid from the saddle and dropped a rein to the ground as Poncho's cue to stand quietly. He'd best not speak until Grace pulled the knife away from the pathetic animal on the ground. Castration was a rough task, but it had to be done with the male calves who'd end up going to market.

But it didn't have to be done by Grace.

After several long minutes, she straightened and scooted back. "He's done." As the men eased the calf's legs down, Antonio stepped in with a bucket of medicine.

Monty focused his gaze on Grace. She squared her shoulders and arched her back in a stretch, still holding her bloody hands in front of her. The outline of her lean form cleared the air from his lungs like a slam to his gut. What was he doing letting a woman—and quite a beautiful one, at that—roll around out here with the cattle? Yet, she sure seemed to be at home with the animals. And seemed to know what she was doing, besides.

He cleared his throat, and Grace eased her head toward him, raising her gaze to meet his. "Yes, sir?"

With those blue eyes studying him, any words he'd planned to speak fled his tongue. "I need you to..." He cleared his throat again. "...switch places with Santiago, roping the calves."

She arched her brows. "But I just rotated to this job." She shot a glance at her helpers, busy wrestling another young bull into place. "And I don't seem to mind it as much as the others."

No surprise that it bothered the men, but they earned good wages to do the work.

"I can do it, Monty."

He met her earnest gaze.

A shout rang out across the pasture. Monty whipped toward the sound in time to see a horse rear and its rider topple to the ground. He ran toward the scene, every muscle tensed. All the men and their horses were seasoned workers. Not likely a horse would rear unless there was danger. Whatever hid in that clump of bushes couldn't be good.

As Monty neared, the green shirt proclaimed the man on the ground to be Santiago. He pushed up to a sitting position and reached toward his leg.

Monty slowed to a walk so he could better find the danger. Nothing that he could see. "Are you hurt?"

"Snake." Santiago's voice came out in a low growl, and Monty followed his gaze to a grey mound that he'd first dismissed as a rock. "I don't have my pistol." Strain laced Santiago's words.

Reaching into his boot, Monty pulled the small Smith & Wesson Model One from the holder he'd rigged there. He cocked the handgun and stepped close enough to ensure his aim. A gun belt was too clumsy when he had to be in and out of the saddle all day, but it was a blessed relief he still carried this smaller pistol.

Monty barely registered the others coming up behind him, but he kept his focus on the reptile coiled less than two feet away from Santiago's boot. Would it strike again? He'd heard of snakes biting more than once if provoked.

The eerie shaking sound of a rattle crept through the air. He didn't have much time. Monty sighted the small pistol, but before his finger could find the trigger, a blast exploded near his right ear.

The snake burst into fifty fragments. Monty whirled, but barely saw the brown blur as someone flew past him to kneel by Santiago's side.

Grace.

She was already pulling Santiago's boot off the leg he clutched. Then her knife was out and she sliced the bottom of his trousers.

Monty forced himself into motion. In two steps he was

kneeling beside her. Santiago's lower leg had already started to swell, and the twin fang marks on his calf loomed a blackish-red. Monty jerked the bandanna from his own neck, and tied it just below the knee. They had to stop the blood from carrying any more venom to the rest of his body.

"Don't cut the wound." Grace's terse comment jerked Monty's attention to her face. "I'm going to make a poultice to draw out the poison."

She knelt by Santiago's head and stroked a soothing hand over his hair, murmuring a few words Monty couldn't decipher. And then she was off, leaving Monty with his dying cousin and a semi-circle of sober-faced men watching him.

Santiago's breathing was already labored, and Monty turned his gaze back to the swollen leg. He'd only done this one other time, and the man had died anyway. Grace said not to cut the wound, something he'd been told to do last time so he could get access to more poison. But she seemed to know what she was about.

Leaning close to the leg, he pressed his mouth to one of the fang marks and sucked, careful to keep his tongue back to block the opening of his throat. The last thing he needed was to swallow the poison himself. With a little liquid in his mouth, he turned his head to the side and spat, then went back to the fang marks. Over and over, he worked to remove the venom.

Was it doing any good? Santiago struggled for breath, groaning, and whiter than any Mexican should look.

Finally Grace reappeared at his side, and the rush of relief that flushed through him took the strength from his muscles. She pressed a damp cloth to Santiago's head, then turned her focus to the leg. After a few seconds of scrutiny, she nodded. "Do you think you got any venom out?"

"Not sure. I didn't cut the wound." Had he ingested some of the poison after all and it was making him light-headed?

"The leg's not as black as I would have expected by now." She worked while she spoke, pouring an oozing mixture on the leg and pressing a bandage to it.

"What's that?"

"Supplies from the chuck wagon. Eggs, salt, and gunpowder. I hope it'll draw the poison out."

"Do you want whiskey?"

"No." Grace spat the word. "Some people think it helps, but I've only seen it make things worse. We'll let this soak in and his body will fight the poison on its own." She glanced at Santiago's face. "We shouldn't move him for a while. Bring blankets and cool water to make him comfortable here. And send someone for the doctor."

Monty turned to Donato, who must have heard Grace's words. He nodded and gripped Nathan's elbow, then the two of them slipped back out of the crowd.

Mama Sarita, their cook, pushed through the men in Donato's wake, and knelt at Santiago's head. She spoke soothing words to the man in Mexican, and stroked a wet cloth over his face. The older woman had been a godsend on the ranch since arriving last year. Born American, she'd married a Mexican man and lived in that country until it was hard to distinguish her from the natives. But when her husband and son died, she'd come back to Texas and taken up cooking for the ranch.

"Can you tie my bandana around this cloth to hold it in place?" Grace's words broke through Monty's stupor.

He took in the scene. Both Grace's hands were occupied with holding the bandage over Santiago's wound so the oozing medicine stayed where it was needed most. His own bandana was still tied tight, just below Santiago's knee. No other extra cloth presented itself.

Monty glanced at Grace's neck and the blue scarf tied there. With Santiago's life possibly hanging in the balance, he shouldn't think twice about reaching for something so near Grace's body. Shouldn't even be thinking about it at all.

"Do it, Monty." Grace had that steel edge to her voice again.

He dropped back on his haunches so he could reach behind her and fumbled with the knot in the fabric. Twice, his fingers brushed the soft skin of her neck, and both times she flinched.

At last, the knot slipped loose, and he pulled the cloth away. He forced his shoulders to relax as he moved back to Grace's side. But as he shifted the bandanna several times around the poultice in Grace's hands, the same clumsiness filled his fingers again. He'd never claimed to be a surgeon, but usually he was pretty good with detailed work. Not this unsteady collection of thumbs that had taken over his fingers.

The inside of his wrist brushed Grace's arm where she'd rolled up her sleeves, and his heart thumped harder in his chest.

Focus, man.

Locking his jaw, he quickly finished the knot, then leaned back and away from Grace.

A loud breath leaked from her. "We'll leave it like that for a while, then check again in a half hour or so." Was it his imagination, or did her voice shake? Of course, this whole ordeal could stretch a person's nerves tight. She'd shown more presence of mind than the rest of them put together.

Monty stood and turned to face the rest of the men. "That's all we can do for now. I reckon', get back to work, but keep the animals away from here."

As the boys wandered back to their duties, Donato appeared with an armful of blankets and a bucket of water.

The women took over, and Monty scooped up a handful of water to rinse his mouth out, just in case any residue of the poison remained. After that, there wasn't much for him to do but stand and watch as they positioned blankets under Santiago's head and continued bathing his face with the cool water. If the man hadn't been so miserable, he'd be a fool not to enjoy the attention.

After a few minutes, Mama Sarita rose to her feet. "I need to check the stew. I'll be back in a bit."

Monty stayed close in case Grace needed him, but he'd never felt more useless. She coddled Santiago and murmured to the man, stroking his face with the towel. He did look a little worse for wear, which kept a lid on Monty's jealousy.

At last Grace turned those blue eyes his way. "Shall we take a look at the bite?"

He swallowed, then nodded and stepped forward.

Grace untied the bandana, her nimble fingers working much better than Monty's had. When she wiped away the poultice mixture, a gruesome sight stared up at them. Blackened skin, swollen to twice its usual size.

"How soon before the doctor arrives?" Grace's quiet words echoed the severity of the picture before them, and sent a stone sinking in Monty's gut.

"Five hours, at the quickest. Prob'ly six."

"I think he should lie still for another half hour, but then we can move him back to the house." She turned to face Monty, and he met her gaze.

Those eyes. So brave and strong, yet it didn't cover the fear there. Monty fought the urge to brush her cheek. "Yes. We can take him in the wagon."

At least getting the wagon ready gave him something productive to do. In just over a half hour, Monty drove the team back toward the ranch house. Mama Sarita had graciously allowed him to move all her cooking supplies out of the chuck wagon into a tent. It'd seemed like the best idea for her to stay with the men and food, while Grace rode in the back with Santiago.

So here he sat. Driving the plodding team, doing his best to avoid the ruts and bumps. Although that was an impossible feat through the prairie land they traveled.

Grace had been quiet behind him. Not unusual for her, but

for some reason the silence bothered him this time. He shot a quick glance behind him, but only saw the back of her head. "How did you learn to tend a rattlesnake bite?"

"Lots of snakes in California. The men were good at listening for them, but we still had at least one bite a year."

"And they brought them to you to tend?"

"I was usually out working with them. Rusty taught me what to do with snakebite. But it doesn't always work."

That he could believe. They'd been blessed with surprisingly few snakes through the years on the Double Rocking B, but he'd read some awful stories in the papers. He couldn't help but hone in on one bit of interesting information she'd shared. "Who's Rusty?"

Silence met his question for a moment, and then finally, "He was our foreman."

"Was?" He almost bit his tongue when the question slipped out. The way she'd said *foreman* with such tenderness sent a surge of warmth through his chest.

Another drop of silence spread between them like ripples in a lake. He fought the urge to turn and study her face.

"He was our foreman from the time I was two years old. Until he died, just before I left California." Grief laced her words.

He wanted to press for more. To ask what this man was like who must have played an important part in her growing up, especially since she'd taken up the cowpuncher's way of life in his footsteps.

But he'd pushed far enough for today. Besides, the affection in her voice told him what kind of man Rusty must have been. The best kind. Someone an impressionable child—and then a determined young woman—had looked up to.

The kind of man Monty wanted to be.

CHAPTER 5

Grace stood in the middle of the yard, one hand resting on her saddle and the other holding Pepper still. Should she stay or go?

Santiago had made it through the night and seemed to be out of the worst of the danger. His leg still had a large area of solid black skin, still swollen, and pretty painful from the look of things. But the doctor had given him a tonic to help with the discomfort, and said it would be best if he slept for the next couple of days.

Monty had ridden back out to the branding camp last night after the doctor left. When Grace had offered to stay at the ranch house overnight to assist the O'Brien family with Santiago's care, Monty had only shrugged and nodded.

But the night had passed now, and she should be joining the other cowpunchers to finish branding. Would Anna be all right caring for Santiago along with her own children? Should she stay and help?

But she'd been hired as a cow hand, not a nurse. Monty hadn't given her leave to shirk her duties with the herd beyond last night.

With a sigh, Grace slipped her boot in the stirrup and vaulted into the saddle. Pepper sidestepped at the motion.

"Easy, girl." The mare settled as Grace relaxed her hold on the reins and fit her other foot into the stirrup. "I guess we're headed out to brand cattle."

~

A week later, Monty herded a group of steers toward the community round-up pens. With a quick reflex, he reined Poncho sideways to cut off a yearling cow's escape. They'd made it to day two of the large round-up with the other ranches, and so far, they'd all kept plenty busy. With night falling soon, it was almost time for some grub.

Up ahead, a cluster of his cowboys sat on horseback outside the corrals. Grace's shapely figure was easy to spot on the outskirts of the group. She sure was shy for a woman, never interacting outside of the Double Rocking B hands. She'd even talked him into letting her stay out of church again this last Sunday, saying she'd remain with Santiago in case he needed assistance.

He still wasn't sure how to feel about her skipping church, although she said she read the Bible on her own. What did she have against gathering with other believers? Should he force her to attend? *Lord, I'd appreciate some guidance here.*

As he herded the cattle closer, Grace looked up, and split from the group, riding out to meet him. Even as exhausted as he was, his pulse picked up a notch at the sight of her coming to see him. Not that she was coming just to enjoy his company, but still...

When she was close enough for those blue eyes to take effect, she asked, "Whose cattle are these?"

Nope, not coming to see him. But at least she'd offered to help. He pointed toward the feisty yearling cow. "That heifer has the Lazy T brand. The rest of 'em can go in Double Rocking B stock."

Grace pointed her mare toward the cow he'd pointed out, and smoothly cut the animal away from the others. As she trailed it toward the Lazy T herd, he couldn't help but watch her go. She knew what she was doing with cattle, no doubt. At least that part of his initial worries could be set aside. But should he still be concerned that she brought danger with her? There'd been no sign of it yet. No threat to the others, anyway. 'Cause she surely did threaten his own concentration when she was around.

But something about Grace still didn't feel right. She was hiding something. Maybe that's why she wouldn't attend church. Was she wanted for a crime? Maybe after round-up he'd head into Seguin and take a look at the posters on the wall in the Post Office. Just to be sure.

A hoot and a string of foul language came from a group of cowboys near the Lazy T herd, jerking Monty's focus toward them. Had the man said what it sounded like? Words that shouldn't be spoken about any woman, much less Grace. And in her presence, too. Grace had neared the group with the heifer, but made no sign of having heard the shout, except for the stiff arch in her back.

Monty turned his focus back to the three cows left in his own little bunch. He had them close to the Double Rocking R herd now, and he motioned for Paco. "Settle these in, will you?"

The cowpuncher moved his horse beside Monty and took over directing the cattle toward the larger group. Monty spun his gelding back toward Grace. She'd already dropped off her charge and rode back in his direction. He met her under the spreading canopy of a grove of pecan trees.

She must have caught the expression on his face, because she reined to a stop in front of him. "Everything all right?"

He had to unclamp his jaw before he could speak. "Did those men say something indecent?"

She shrugged but dropped her gaze. "I can ignore it."

"No." He forced a breath in before he exploded. "I won't have my hands treated disrespectfully."

That made her look at him. Yet, the look wasn't grateful, more wary. "I'd rather not make a stir."

She'd rather be spoken to like a woman in a bawdy house than raise a commotion? Not on his guard. "Go put away your horse." He kicked Poncho forward.

As he neared the cluster of rowdies, Monty took their measure. Jared Thomas usually hired decent cowhands, but this scruffy trio didn't fit that bill. They must be day hands hired for round-up.

He reined in about ten feet in front of the man in the middle. He was pretty sure this was the cad who'd said those things to Grace, and the roguish grin on his leathery face tended to confirmed it.

Monty met the man's gaze with a glare. "Did you call my ranch hand a prostitute?"

The man's greasy yellow mustache twitched. "She's someone I'd pay money to see more of."

The blood boiled in Monty's chest. "If you come near her again, I'll make sure you see the inside of a jail cell. Hands off. She's to be treated with respect."

The other man's eyes narrowed. "Why do you get all the fun?"

Oh, if he could have wrung the scrawny man's neck… "She works with the cattle, nothing more. Stay clear of her or you'll answer to me."

He spun Poncho away and spurred him into a lope before he did something he would regret. Or maybe he wouldn't regret it. The greasy rat probably needed a good pounding. *I'll apologize for that thought later, Lord.* But if the man so much as looked twice at Grace again, he'd find the Lazy T foreman and make sure this lout received a swift dismissal.

The rest of the evening passed in relative peace, with the boys enjoying their normal banter. They brought Grace into the teasing occasionally—always with an undertone of respect—and she was good at giving it right back.

Jesse's pot of beans hadn't been half bad as trail grub, especially with the biscuits Mama Sarita sent. Sleeping on the ground for so many nights would have been too hard on the older woman, so the boys took turns cooking meals during the round-up.

As they settled into tents and bedrolls, the night sounds took over. Crickets. The occasional low bellow of a cow. Monty pulled a blanket over himself, and adjusted his head against his saddle. Not such a comfortable pillow. A lot of the men—and Grace—slept under canvas tents, but he'd always preferred the open air. It let him keep an eye on things, and made him feel a bit closer to God without anything shielding him from the Lord's creation.

Lord, I'm not sure why things are feeling so off-kilter these days. Guide me. And with the prayer in his heart, his eyes drifted shut.

~

Something wasn't right.

Monty eased his head over to peer into the darkness without creating a sound from his movement. Everything seemed still. The stars had all bedded down for the night, leaving only the moon to watch over the darkest part of the night when men and animals slept peacefully.

There again. The white sides of a tent fluttered, as if something pushed it from inside. He focused on the movement. That was Grace's tent.

Monty sat up. Should he go see if something was wrong? It

couldn't be proper for him to see her sleeping, yet if she needed something... Maybe she was having a nightmare, or one of those epileptic fits he'd read about in the paper.

He sprang to his feet and crept toward the tent. Something was definitely moving around in there. Thrashing, it looked like. Should he call out to wake her from the nightmare? But he didn't want to disturb the others. And it could be a bit embarrassing for Grace. No matter how polite, the boys wouldn't be able to resist a little teasing.

Stopping at the edge of the tent, he hooked his fingers around the flap, but didn't pull. "Grace," he whispered, just loud enough for her to hear if she were awake.

A muffled sound came from the tent, but the thrashing stopped. Then a quiet squeal and...a man's voice? Monty jerked the flap aside.

His eyes locked on the business end of the pistol pointed straight at him.

He fought the urge to step back as he took in the scene. A man—the blond thug from the Lazy T—held the gun in one hand and the other clamped over Grace's mouth.

The look in her eyes sank in Monty's gut like a rock in water. Utter fear. He jerked his attention back to the man as his mind spun through his options.

He'd not stopped to grab his Colt, and the Smith and Wesson in his boot was too far from reach. If the bloke would just lose his focus for half a second, Monty could dive in and get the upper hand.

His gaze flickered back to Grace for only an instant. Her hands pressed against the ground, but it didn't look like they were tied. Why didn't she try to get away? Maybe he could signal her to create a distraction.

"She already knows if she makes a move, you'll die first, then her." The man's voice came out hard as steel, not the jeering tone from earlier that day. "But I'd surely prefer to enjoy this pretty lady instead."

An almost imperceptible movement came from Grace's direction, as if she were shrinking away. But Monty kept his full focus on the adversary.

"So, mister, now that you ruined our party, I reckon you'll need to step aside whilst we move the fun elsewhere."

Over his dead body.

"I said *move*." The man turned the pistol from Monty toward Grace, but it was the distraction Monty needed.

The moment the barrel shifted toward the air, he charged the man. Slamming into the thug's chest, he grabbed the gun arm with one hand and his throat with the other.

The gun exploded.

The man scrambled, but Monty's reactions were honed from dealing with too many ornery cows. He had the man on his stomach within seconds, both hands twisted behind his back.

Only then did he glance up at Grace. She was so far in the dark recesses of the tent, he could only make out her huddled profile. "Are you all right?"

"Y-yes. The bullet grazed me, but it's not bad." Her voice was so weak, it took him a moment for the words to register.

She'd been hit? His muscles bunched to run to her, but he had to keep a firm grip on the man underneath him.

"What happened, boss?" Donato stood at the tent's opening.

Thank you, Lord. "This blighter attacked Grace. Tie him tight and get him ready for jail. And send someone for the doctor. Grace was hit by that shot." A crash of guilt poured over him. The man never would have fired if Monty hadn't moved.

"I don't need a doctor. It just skinned me." Grace's voice was a little stronger this time.

Monty rolled off the man on the ground as Donato took over. While his cousin yelled commands to the men gathering outside the tent, Monty focused all is attention on Grace.

She was balled in a corner of the little canvas covering, almost hidden in the dark shadows.

"Let me see it." He tried to gentle his tone, but so much anger still coursed through his veins.

"Monty, please. I just want to be left alone." Half-whisper, half-cry, the words pierced him.

"Grace." He wanted to take her in his arms and make everything all right. But he stayed put.

Donato finally dragged the grimy lout out of the tent, amidst a string of curses from the scoundrel.

Silence took over, and Monty's eyes finally adjusted to the darkness. He touched the elbow below where Grace clutched her upper arm. "Let me put salve on it and make sure you don't need stitches."

She let out a shaky breath. "All right."

He stepped out of the tent and over to the cooking supplies where the medicines were kept. After lighting a lantern, the salve and bandages were easy enough to find.

"We're takin' him in now. You want the doc to come?" Donato met Monty halfway back to Grace's tent.

Monty's glance roamed the canvas, then back to his cousin's face. "She says it's not bad enough to need him. I suppose if it is, she should go to the clinic anyway. Just see that *canalla* gets locked up."

"Got it."

When Monty crouched back inside the tent, Grace had moved away from the corner. She sat in the middle of the space, clutching her shirt around her.

He'd never seen her so...vulnerable. Always before, she'd had a competent air about her. But now, fear spread across her features in tight lines and haunted eyes.

Monty knelt beside her, and Grace drew back from him. *Easy now.*

She looked like she might bolt any minute. Had that man

done something to her? His gaze flickered to her white-knuckled grip on her shirt. There was a button missing near where she held it closed.

"Grace." The whispered word escaped before he could stop it. "Did he…touch you?"

Her gaze met his, then skittered away. "No, Monty. Please… just look at my arm. I want this all to end."

The pleading in her voice tightened his gut. He focused on her left arm where a bloody circle stood out against the brown of her shirt. The fabric was torn in a line across her arm, and he eased the edges back.

She was right, it was mostly a deep scratch. The bleeding had already tapered off, and it didn't look bad enough for stitches. He wiped away the blood with a clean bandage, then applied a healthy dose of salve.

His gaze flickered to her face, sinking into her blue eyes as they studied him. He swallowed, as much to draw moisture into his mouth as to focus on his task. "It would do best if it were wrapped."

"I'll do it." She spoke quickly.

He glanced at the wound again. Even if she didn't manage to secure a bandage around it, keeping salve on the wound should be enough for it to heal. And tomorrow he'd send her back to the ranch where Anna and Mama Sarita could look after her.

He should have known better than to let his guard down around those roughnecks. Grace had depended on him, and he'd let her down.

He couldn't let that happen again.

CHAPTER 6

Grace slipped the last button in place on her vest, then checked her holster again. She desperately hoped that was coffee she smelled, not just leftover wood smoke.

What a night. She'd not slept much after that blackguard attacked her. It had helped that Monty'd said he'd be right outside her tent if she needed him. Still, every time she'd closed her eyes, she saw the vile man's greasy face or smelled his rank body odor. How could his touch be so permanently seared into her skin?

Pushing to her feet, Grace pulled the tent flap aside and stepped out. At least she had work to keep her mind and body occupied today.

Monty was crouched by the fire, talking with Carlos and Donato, but he rose when he saw her. He had a tin coffee cup in each hand, and stepped forward to offer one to her.

She took it in both hands, cupping her fingers around the warmth. "Exactly what I needed. Thanks." She sipped the dark brew. Oh, was it good. A vast improvement over the stuff they'd had to drink the last two days. "This is better than usual."

"Thanks."

She looked up to find him watching her. "You made it?"

"I did." The corners of his mouth played like he was trying to smile, but the creases under his eyes would have none of it. He looked…haggard. Which made him even more handsome, if that were possible.

Her eyes begged to look away, but she forced herself to hold his gaze. "You don't look so good. Are you all right this morning?" That wasn't quite what she'd meant to say.

He quirked a brow. "You're asking *me* if I'm all right?"

Heat seeped up her neck, and she glanced down into her coffee. "Anyway, thanks for the help last night."

"I'm just sorry it happened."

"Yeah, me too." She kicked at a clump of dirt. But she was more than ready to forget about the attack. Leave the night behind them. Grace glanced toward the fire. "Anything for breakfast?"

Monty stepped aside, revealing a pot in the coals. "Warmed beans and leftover biscuits."

She fought hard to keep her grimace from showing. One thing she'd never gotten use to was trail grub. The stuff got nastier the longer they were away. "Thanks." She crouched down to fill a plate with beans. "Which way do you want me to head out today?"

"Back to the ranch."

Jerking her gaze up to his, she almost fell back on her rear. "The round-up goes three more days. Why are we leaving early?" Surely it wasn't because of the run-in last night. No rancher in his right mind would give up so many cattle because of an altercation with another ranch's hired man.

"Not all of us." His voice gentled a little, but there was a steel undertone to it. "Just you. Donato will ride back with you and pick up more supplies."

She straightened as fast as her weary legs would lift her, pulling to her full height and squaring her shoulders. Unfortunately, she was still a good six inches shy of his large frame. "Why? I'm being punished because that scoundrel made trouble? I suppose you think I started the whole mess."

"Grace. No, I..." He turned away, and she couldn't read his expression. "You need to let your arm heal. Take a few days off."

She stepped around so he had to look at her. "I've had deeper nicks from freeing a tangled calf. I'm fine."

He didn't answer, but he wouldn't look her in the eyes either.

Frustration coursed through her. "What's really the problem here, Monty? Have I not proven myself fit as a cowhand? You think I'm unreliable? A danger to the other men and animals?"

He turned back to the fire—away from Grace—and scrubbed a hand through his hair. Finally, he exhaled a long sigh. "I guess you can stay. But keep close to your partner and *don't* wander off alone."

She studied his profile. Why was that fiasco last night bothering him so? It was *her* life. Why should it affect his peace of mind? Unless he just wanted to get her out of his hair.

But something about the drawn expression on his face didn't say frustration. More like...a mild version of torture. Should she push to understand why? Or leave him be? He'd said she could stay, so shouldn't she leave well enough alone?

Stepping forward she rested her fingers on his arm. "Monty?"

He flinched, and a muscle in his jaw flexed. "What." He looked like he might explode any moment.

Maybe best leave it be for now. "Who should I partner with today?"

That muscle in his jaw shifted again. "Donato."

With that, she stepped back and retreated toward the horses.

But when she'd almost finished saddling her mare, she glanced back to the campfire. Monty stood rooted in the spot she'd left him, staring into the cooling ashes.

Her chest ached to go to him. To slip her arms around his

waist and take comfort there—to give comfort. But instead, she picked up the bridle and fit it into Pepper's mouth.

She had no business getting too close to anyone here. As much as she wanted to stay, if Leonard found her, she'd have no choice but to flee. And caring about the people from the Double Rocking B would only make things harder when she had to leave.

~

When round-up finally ended on Friday, Grace had never been so glad to see the grand log home and outbuildings of the Double Rocking B. She didn't mind long days in the saddle, but she'd missed coming back to a soft bed every night.

Monty was kind enough to give the whole crew the day off on Saturday, and most of them—including Monty—headed into town.

But that was the last place Grace could go. She'd much rather be snuggled here in the rocking chair holding baby Martin, while Anna worked a puzzle on the side table with her daughter Emmaline. Anna, of course, wanted to know all the details of the run-in with that lout from the Lazy T.

When Grace finished the tale, Anna leaned back in her chair. "I'll bet Monty was fit to be tied." She gave a dry chuckle, but then her face sobered. "I'm just glad you weren't seriously hurt. None of us would have forgiven ourselves, especially Monty."

Grace studied Anna's face as the other woman stared at the puzzle pieces. "Monty seems...protective."

Anna glanced up. "That's one way to put it." She met Grace's gaze. "I'm not sure if it came from losing his parents so young, or if the drive to protect was just born into him. As long as I've known Monty though, he's been fiercely loyal. I think he takes a bit too much of the burden on his own shoulders, but there's no way to stop him."

A hint of a smile quirked one side of Anna's mouth. "I think that's why he was so upset when I hired you without seeking his opinion. He thought you'd somehow bring trouble to the ranch, and he hadn't had the chance to properly determine your experience and background."

Grace fought to keep her face impassive. Would Monty have ferreted out her secret if she'd spoken with him first? Or not even given her a second glance?

And what if she *did* bring danger to the ranch? Leonard could be so volatile, and if he found her here, he wouldn't think twice of destroying anything in his path to get what he sought. She swallowed down the lump in her throat, then glanced at Anna.

The other woman watched her, curiosity in her gaze, but concern too. "I think he's settled into the idea of you working here. You're on the inside now, part of those he'll protect."

That was the worst news Anna could have shared. Bumps broke out on Grace's arms as an image of Leonard's furious face filled her mind. He may not be as big and strong as Monty, but her step-brother would have no qualms about killing any man who got in the way. He'd already done it once, although she couldn't prove it.

"Are you all right, Grace? You look a bit pale."

Grace blinked and brought her focus back to Anna. "I'm fine." She looked down at the baby sleeping in her lap. Even closed, Martin's eyelids flickered as though some wild dream played behind them. Every so often, his mouth would pucker or his chubby little foot would kick. "He doesn't stop moving does he?"

"Don't I know it."

Grace glanced up to share the smile in Anna's tone.

The young mother gazed at the child with tired adoration.

"He keeps me on my toes. It'll be hard with Jacob gone on business to San Antonio next week. But at least I have Mama Sarita. She helps a lot." The woman's face perked. "And Bo. Did I tell you Monty's brother, Bo, is bringing his family to see us for a few days?"

Grace raised her brows. "Really? Do they live nearby?"

"Two counties north of us. Bo works on a ranch up there, so we don't get to see them much. Did you know Bo used to work here with Monty?"

Grace shook her head. So much new information today. Her picture of Monty shifted with each piece.

"Yes, Bo was here when I first came. Stayed for about five years after that, then set out to make his own way. I think he felt like he'd always be under Monty's shadow if he stayed here. Anyway, he did well for himself. Worked up to foreman on the ranch he's at now, found a wife, and now has two of the prettiest children you'll ever see." Anna tapped her own daughter's chin. "Except for these two, of course. Emmy's excited about Paul and Sandria coming, aren't you, honey?"

Emmaline nodded and cut a shy smile at Grace. The child had been remarkably quiet through the whole conversation, maybe because she wasn't comfortable in Grace's presence yet. They'd have to work on that.

"Oh, Grace. I've been meaning to tell you. I went through my wardrobe and took out some dresses that I'll never be able to wear again after having these two." She nodded toward her children. "If you want to try them, you're welcome to."

Unease filtered through Grace as she eyed her shirtwaist and baggy trousers. "I did bring one dress, but I've been saving it for a special occasion. I'm sure you'd rather me wear skirts on my days off."

Anna waved the comment away. "Whatever you're comfortable with is fine around the ranch." Her mouth pinched in a grin. "When you go to town, though, a skirt might be best if you don't want the old ladies to swoon."

And that, Grace definitely didn't want. The less attention she drew to herself, the better. Of course, she wouldn't be going to town at all if she could help it.

CHAPTER 7

Grace sloshed through the mud as she followed the rope to the calf on the ground. Georgina had pulled him from the thick mud, but he still wasn't getting up. Maybe just worn out, but she needed to make sure. No mother cow hovered nearby. This must be one of the foundlings.

As the mist changed to a steady rain again, Grace pushed the dripping strands of hair from her face and crouched in front of the little fellow. It'd been raining for two days now. Nothing at all like the dry California desert. She loosened her rope and lifted it over the calf's body. "Come on, fella. Let's get you over to your friends where it's not so muddy."

She scrubbed the calf in a rough rubdown to get the blood flowing again, and it finally struggled to its feet. The little legs were shaky at first, but after a few steps, he trotted off to the herd.

Grace wiped the worst of the mud from her hands onto the grass, then straightened and trudged back to Georgina. As she stood by the horse, gathering the rope into even loops, Monty appeared through the fog and drizzle.

"Time to head in," he called. "Let's get out of this mess."

She nodded. There wasn't much she'd rather do right now than eat a warm dinner, or maybe take an even warmer bath. Lord willing.

Monty settled his horse into step beside hers as they rode toward the pack of soggy cowpunchers and the trail home.

When the ranch buildings came into sight, Juan and his stable boy, Chester, met them at the barn, taking horses and offering dry towels to the weary cow hands.

"Everyone clean up before you head in for dinner." Monty shouted the command over the rain on the tin roof as he unsaddled his gelding.

A few of the men grumbled under their breath, but Grace couldn't tell if it was from Monty's words or the fact they were all muddy and miserable. Messy evenings like this seemed a good reason not to feed the cow punchers in the main house. But who was she to argue? Certainly not the boss's daughter anymore.

After settling Georgina in the corral and drying her supplies, Grace made a run for the big house. Rain fell in big pellets, and her clothing that had dried in the barn soaked through again.

On the shelter of the porch, she eased off her hat so it didn't drip water down her back, then tried to wipe the mud off her boots. There was no chance of it. She'd sunk to her ankles more times than she could count, and the sludge was impossible to scrape off. Mr. O'Brien was still gone on his business trip, so maybe it would be best to remove the boots on the porch. She could hurry upstairs. And even if someone saw her in her stockinged feet, it would only be the women or children.

After leaning against the log siding to remove her boots, she set them on the far corner of the porch. Maybe no one would notice them there.

With hat in hand, she opened the front door and tiptoed inside. She'd made it almost to the stairs when footsteps sounded on the landing above. She thought about ducking into a room, but held her ground. It would only be Anna or Mama Sarita.

But it wasn't.

As she stood, soaked and disheveled at the bottom of the stairs, a man appeared at the top.

A man? Her heart kicked into a gallop and her muscles bunched to run. But he bore no resemblance to Leonard, more like the dark features of the cow hands she worked with every day.

He stopped when he saw her, then tilted his chin and raised a single brow. "Hello." It was almost a question, and rightly so. He had to be wondering what a soaking wet woman was doing climbing the stairs in trousers and stockings. But who was he?

And then like a punch, his identity hit her. Monty's brother. Anna said he'd be arriving with his family this week. Heat crept up her neck, and flooded her face. "Hello, I…uh…was just going to freshen up."

His mouth quirked, and he stepped to the side of the upstairs landing, motioning for her to precede him. "By all means."

Should she run for the kitchen? Or try to make it up the stairs—past Monty's brother—and into her room, without him getting a close look at her bedraggled state. She didn't have dry clothes in the kitchen, and the damage here was pretty much done. She might as well take the second option.

With her chin high and every bit of the regal bearing her mother tried to teach her, Grace ascended the stairs and swept past the man on the upper landing. When she made it inside her room—down the right hall and through the second door—Grace pressed the door closed and sank against it.

Company. Today of all days. When she dripped water like a drowned prairie dog and every muscle ached from fighting mud all day.

But she didn't have time to stop. She'd be expected at dinner soon and she had a lot of cleaning up to do.

~

"How was the ride in?" Monty clasped his brother's hand in the front parlor.

"Wet." Bo's grin said maybe it had been worth it, though.

"No doubt." He chuckled and leaned forward to kiss his sister-in-law's cheek. "Good to see you, Miranda. Where'd you hide my niece and nephew?" But he needn't have asked. Paul's two-year-old voice rang through the house, rising over the sound of the cow hands filtering into the dining room.

Miranda offered a tight smile. "You get three guesses. Paul's hard to lose with that loud voice."

Anna, ever poised with her Southern belle charm, propped the baby on her hip and stepped forward to take Miranda's elbow. "Dinner should be ready now. Let's all head that way. I'm just sorry Jacob couldn't be here to welcome y'all. We expect him back tomorrow, though."

Monty fell into step with Bo behind the ladies, and eyed his brother as they headed toward the parlor doorway. "Looks like the northern counties have been good to you. Or maybe family life."

A grin spread over Bo's face and he dropped his voice, slowing as they neared the main hall. "Things are good, Monty. Real good. Miranda's expecting again, too."

The words punched like a right hook to his gut. He tried not to let the pain register on his face. Three children. Bo had a beautiful wife and soon to be three children, and Monty couldn't find a woman to save his soul. What was wrong with him?

But he forced out the expected words. "That's great, Bo. I'm real happy for you. You deserve it." And Bo did deserve it. But that didn't stop the loneliness from gripping his gut and twisting.

They rounded the corner into the long hallway that spanned

the house from front to back, and a flash of blue on the stairs caught Monty's attention.

A woman descended with all the regal airs of a princess.

Grace?

She wore a dress the color of a spring sky, with puffy layers cascading down the front and ruffled sleeves. And her hair… Styled up in a pouf on top of her head instead of the usual braid, it outlined the elegant length of her neck.

She was breathtaking. Truly. His chest constricted, not allowing a bit of air in.

His eyes roamed up to her face. She was near enough he could see those crystal blue eyes—deepened by the same shade in the dress. And they were locked on his. A hint of a smile played across her mouth as she reached the bottom of the stairs.

Something poked his side hard enough to knock him off balance. Monty glanced over to see Bo's teasing half-grin, just a little too close. A single brow raised on his kid brother's face.

Monty swallowed. He should probably make introductions. "Bo, I'd like you to meet Grace—Miss Harper." He swept his gaze to Grace and fell into her smile as she stepped closer. "Grace, my brother…" But he couldn't take his eyes from her. Where had the muddy cowpuncher gone? She was more elegant than any woman he'd seen.

Now that she was close enough, he could see the ear bobs dangling from her delicate lobes. Light blue stones, almost the color of those sparkling eyes. She extended a dainty hand in Bo's direction. "It's a pleasure to meet you, Mr.…Dominguez?" She looked to Monty, but he could only stare at her. The way the light danced in her eyes. Her full lips…

"Yes, ma'am. The pleasure is mine." Bo took the extended fingers, bowing low. When had his baby brother learned ballroom manners? "You must be the new cowpuncher Anna told us about. I'm sure you've had your hands full keeping my brother here in line."

Monty had an itch to knock the twinkle out of Bo's eye. "I think they're waiting for us at the table." He stepped forward between the two of them, elbowing Bo aside. For a second, he almost extended his arm to escort Grace into the dining room. But a shy awkwardness took over, and he waved her forward instead. "After you."

What was he doing? This wasn't the cowhand he'd worked beside these last few weeks. How in the world was he supposed to treat her now, decked out and stunning in this dress? He'd never been trail boss to a lady before.

A bit of the conversation in the dining room died away as Grace entered, but the boys had the good sense not to leave their jaws hanging open too long.

Monty motioned toward Bo, hoping a little distraction would help. "Most of you fellows remember my brother, Bo."

Donato was the first to step forward and give Bo a hearty slap on the back. "Good to see you, *primo*." Good ol', Donato.

But over Bo's shoulder, Donato sent Monty a wink and raised a brow toward Grace, as if to say, "Sweet molasses, did you see her?"

I know, primo. I know. It was all Monty could do not to watch her glide across the room to her chair.

No doubt about it. He was in trouble.

~

It was only mid-afternoon the next day when Grace caught sight of Santiago waving her in. She'd been riding the edge of the herd, watching for young calves straying too far from safety, but it looked like the rest of the men were headed toward the trail back to the ranch.

Surely they weren't done for the day already. They still had a couple hours before quitting time. Of course, the rain hadn't let up. Was it normal to have this much rain in Texas? Seemed like a miserable way to spend the spring.

She reined in her horse when she reached Santiago.

"Boss says we're headed in early. Reckon he'd rather see his brother than look at a bunch of drenched cattle."

Grace nodded and fell in line behind Santiago. She couldn't say she blamed him. Bo seemed like a good-humored, likable man, and his wife, Miranda, had such a sweet spirit about her. And Miranda had confided last night that they had another baby on the way. The joy that lit her face with the whispered announcement had started a longing in Grace's chest. Would she ever have the opportunity for a family of her own?

At twenty-eight, she would well be considered an old maid. Wouldn't Mama be horrified? Mama had been working hard to prepare her for matrimony before her death almost a decade before, but after that...

Grace had wanted nothing more than to work with the animals, alongside Papa and Rusty. The foolish trappings of courting and social events among the neighboring ranches seemed like a waste of time.

And now, even if she did take a husband, she'd have to give up the work she'd come to love. Would it be worth it? At least it would get her out of this miserable rain. And the more time she spent with the children, the more the longings crept in. But it couldn't even be an option now. Not until she was free of Leonard.

As the ranch buildings came into view, she shook off the melancholy thoughts. A wagon sat in front of the barn with several figures hustling around it. Had Mr. O'Brien returned? He'd taken a wagon with him to pick up supplies. What a wet ride home he would have had.

Indeed it was Mr. O'Brien. He waved at the cowpunchers riding in as he jogged through the rain toward the house.

Grace took her time unsaddling her mare in the barn,

brushing Pepper and rubbing her down with a rag. She wasn't exactly avoiding going inside, but the barn was so peaceful with the drum of rain on the roof and the loamy smell of wet dirt and animals. If she were warm and dry, she would have camped out here for the rest of the day.

But instead, she settled Pepper into a stall and headed toward the house. As she stepped through the front door, a cluster of voices drifted from the dining room. Were they having coffee and a snack? Maybe some of Mama Sarita's dried apple pie. Sounded perfect for a day like today.

She was able to sneak up the stairs without meeting anyone, and exhaled a long breath as she closed her bedroom door. What she wouldn't give for a bath. But that was out of the question with so many people around, so she'd have to settle for another thorough wipe down with a damp cloth like last night.

A glimpse of green on the bed snagged her attention. Grace stepped forward and examined the two gowns laid out on the quilt. The one on top was a forest green taffeta, with darker green and white lace trimming, and the gown underneath was a lovely burgundy muslin. She fingered the lace on the green dress. These must be ones Anna had said she'd pass along.

The ladies had carried on last night about her blue gown, the only one she'd folded in her bedroll before she left California. After wearing trousers for so many months straight, it had felt strange to be in a skirt again, yet comfortable at the same time. Like a pair of old cotton drawers, softened from many washings, yet just discovered hiding at the bottom of the wardrobe.

And the way Monty had looked at her... As much as she shouldn't have enjoyed his attention, she had. Even now, she replayed the scene in her mind. The way his dark eyes rounded, then darkened to a smolder. The play of a smile at his mouth. The show of possessiveness when any of the other men spoke to her.

But possessiveness? That couldn't be what it was. Protection. Yes, Monty and his fierce desire to protect.

After removing as much mud and grime as she could, Grace slipped into clean underthings, then pulled the green dress into place. It actually fit fairly well. A little tight through the chest, but not unbearable or too obvious. Maybe later, she could let out the seams.

Staring at herself in the mirror, she twisted her hair up and held it in place, trying to envision herself through Monty's eyes. Of course, last night was the first time he'd seen her in anything other than grubby cowpuncher clothes. Had he finally realized she was a woman? A better question was…did she want him to?

No.

She dropped her hair like a hot branding iron. It was important she be seen as an equal in the man's world she'd joined. Tough enough to withstand the rigors of life with longhorns.

But when she fastened her hair in the usual long braid, it didn't look right with the dress. So she settled for gathering it into a low ribbon, pulled to the side to give just a touch of elegance. Being braided all morning had left her hair in loose curls as it dried from the rain.

Another glimpse in the mirror made her pause. Good enough? Her ears looked lonely, but she wasn't wearing Mama's blue zircon earrings again. That had been too much last night. Yet dressing up had been as natural as breathing. When guests were present, she was expected to represent the family well.

But she wasn't part of this family, and she had no role to play, except as hired cowhand.

Slipping out the door, she headed for the stairs. It was too early to convene in the dining room, but with the added guests, Mama Sarita might need a hand with the meal. It was a wonder the woman could cook such feasts every day.

As she descended the stairs, the sound of excited male voices drifted from the parlor. The muscles in her shoulders tensed until she was able to detect each of them.

Mr. O'Brien. Bo. Monty.

When her slippered foot touched the bottom landing, Grace tiptoed around the bannister and headed straight for the kitchen.

Even knowing she could trust these men, the less stir she made, the better.

CHAPTER 8

"You should have seen it, Monty. Right there in the Alamo Plaza."

Monty leaned back in the armchair and watched Jacob wave his hands dramatically while he told of the happenings in San Antonio. He'd not seen his friend this animated in quite a while.

"A whole herd of longhorns, pressing and straining against the barbed wire. But it didn't budge. Not one of them got through." Jacob sank against his chair back, apparently exhausted. Or maybe just awestruck. "I ordered enough to fence along the north pasture for now. If we like it, we'll get more."

Monty sat straighter. "You ordered it already?"

"Yep. You'll love it, Monty. Wait and see."

Love it? That was quite a strong emotion to apply to thin strands of spiked wire. He picked up the six inch sample Jacob had brought and examined the piece. Glidden's Winner Wire, they'd called it.

"McManus said it has a reputation for being light as air, stronger than whiskey, and cheap as dirt." Jacob raised a hand, palm out. "His words, not mine."

Monty dropped the wire back in his lap and turned to his brother. "You guys use anything like this?"

Bo shook his head. "No. I can see where it'd help keep track of the cattle though."

Jacob leaned forward, gripping the arms of his chair. "You should've seen the way ranchers were placing orders for the stuff. I was one of the first in line, though. Said we should receive delivery in a couple of weeks."

Monty eased out a long breath. Only a couple of weeks? Something about this didn't sit well in his gut. But Jacob was so excited about the idea. And he'd already purchased the wire. The decision had been taken out of Monty's hands, but he'd have to make the best of it.

~

"Dodger has very bright eyes and he does many funny things." Grace sat on the kitchen floor, her back against the wall. Emmaline and Sandria balanced on each of her legs, both girls holding a side of *McGuffey's Second Eclectic Reader* so Grace could read the stories to them. "He likes to put his paws up on the crib and watch the baby."

Emmaline giggled. "If we had a dog, I bet it would do that to Martin's crib. And Mama would say, 'Get down.'"

Grace chuckled. "I'll bet you're right."

Mama Sarita sent them a tender smile from where she stirred something in a pot at the stove.

"We have a dog. He likes to lick me." Four-year-old Sandria's nose wrinkled as she spoke. "He likes Papa too, but not Paul. Paul pulls hair and hurts."

Such cute little angels, these two. Grace scanned the book to find her place, but the door opened beside them, dragging her attention upward. She expected to see Miranda, fresh from her nap with Paul. Instead, her gaze landed on a pair of grey trousers. She raised her focus up, up…to Monty's lean torso, broad shoulders, and finally his chiseled face.

His gaze met hers as surprise flashed across his features. He looked to each of the girls, then back to her, up to Mama Sarita, around the room, then back to Grace again. "I…was coming to see if we had any coffee left."

"Uncle Monty!" Both girls clamored the words as they scrambled to their feet.

Grace winced as they stumbled over her outstretched skirts and ankles. As soon as they were clear, they launched themselves into Monty's legs. Squeals erupted as he lumbered forward, lifting each girl as they clung tight to a leg. "Oh ho, seems like my legs have grown creatures." He deepened his voice like a giant, then braced one hand against the wall and raised the opposite leg in the air, giving it a sound shake.

Emmaline's giggle rattled as she clutched his knee for dear life. "No, stop." But her request was almost swallowed up in laughter.

Monty lowered that leg and raised the other. "That creature won't get off. Let's see about this one."

Sandria was already laughing, but when she soared upward with Monty's leg, a little squeal broke loose, followed by a chorus of giggles.

It was impossible not to laugh with so many happy sounds filling the room. She'd never seen this playful side of Monty. Sure, he would joke or tease with the men, especially around the campfire when they'd camped out during branding and roundup. But nothing like this jovial uncle, who now scooped both girls up—one in each arm—and raised them upside down over his shoulders.

The grin spreading across his face made her stomach flip, and something in her chest craved to have him focus that smile on her. Gone were the tired lines around his eyes from sun and wind and work. Why didn't he have a family of his own, with sons and daughters he could laugh and play with every day? Surely a man with Monty's rugged good looks and quiet wisdom would have every unmarried woman in town setting her sights on him. So why hadn't he settled down?

And then he swung around, turning those handsome dark eyes her direction. "Are you girls behaving for Miss Grace? Showing her how you can be young ladies?"

Grace raised her brows at him. After he'd just flown them about, hanging upside down and jiggling until their teeth loosened, he was worried about them acting like young ladies? She sent a grin to each girl. "We've been having a grand time, but I can tell my reading isn't quite as fun as playing with Uncle Monty."

Sandria wiggled in Monty's arms until he lowered her to the ground. She ran over to Grace and placed a hand on her shoulder. With a solemn expression she said, "Your reading was very good, Miss Grace."

Grace couldn't help but pull the tender-hearted girl into a hug. "Thank you, Sandria. You made it special." Her gaze caught Monty's over the child's shoulder, and his face wore an unusual expression. Almost like confusion, but not quite. Something in her stomach clenched.

"Here Emmy-belle, let your Uncle Monty sit and drink his coffee." Mama Sarita's words broke through the moment, and Monty turned away to the table where the older woman placed a mug.

But as his attention left her, a wave of loneliness replaced it. Enough. She couldn't be a sappy-eyed female. She was here to do a job. A man's job. And it would take all her energy and focus to do it well. Monty was a distraction she couldn't afford.

~

Conversation at the dinner table that night centered around Mr. O'Brien's news from San Antonio. Barbed wire? Grace had heard of it from Papa, of course, but he'd said it wouldn't be a viable option. How much wire would it take to fence in five hundred acres? And would the stuff really keep the cattle contained?

The tale Mr. O'Brien told of the demonstration certainly sounded fantastic. The men peppered him with questions, but she couldn't help but notice Monty's silence. In fact, he didn't speak a word until Nathan asked him how they were going to get the fences built.

In his usual deliberate way, Monty paused before answering, which brought the entire room to a hush as they awaited his response. "I guess we'll split off a crew to work on the fence, while the rest keep going with our other work. We'll rotate one person out each day so everyone gets a chance to build fences. We can start with four men, then see how it goes."

"How soon 'til the wire gets here?" Santiago aimed the question at Mr. O'Brien, and the attention of the room swung back to that end of the table.

Grace continued to watch Monty, though. He dipped his head to eat a bite of enchilada, and when he raised it again, twin lines creased his forehead. He definitely didn't seem to share Mr. O'Brien's enthusiasm for the project. What were his concerns? In theory, it sounded like a good idea to enclose the ranch's property. It would likely take less manpower to care for the herd, and be easier to keep track of the cattle. Not to mention keeping unwanted animals out.

Was Monty upset because he was left out of the decision, and now being saddled with the task of getting the work done? But that didn't feel right either. Maybe she could find a quiet moment later to ask.

~

Monty stepped onto the front porch and eased the door shut behind him. The rain had finally stopped, and the clouds parted in areas to reveal twinkling stars. Inside, the house had started to feel cramped and stuffy with all those people. He needed a few minutes to himself. And the fresh, after-rain smell in the night air was perfect.

He settled onto the porch rail, his back against a post, and stared out at the grassy expanse surrounding the house. Only thirty feet or so was visible before it faded into the darkness beyond. What would it be like for all this open land to be fenced?

The door behind him creaked, and light spilled onto the porch floor.

Monty didn't move. Most of the cowpunchers had already headed to the bunkhouse, but maybe one or two of his cousins had stayed to reminisce about old times with Bo, and were now headed for bed.

A soft swish sounded. Not the thud of boots on wood.

He turned for a glance over his shoulder, and his pulse skipped a beat. Grace.

She stepped toward him, wrapping her arms around her against the chill of the spring night. He tracked her movements with his gaze, but when she stopped beside him and stared into the night, he did the same.

"I'm not used to seeing you in a dress." He kept his voice quiet so he didn't disturb the sounds of nature.

"It's been a while since I've worn one. But Anna gave me this, and I thought it best with company in the house." She sounded subdued, and he couldn't tell if wearing the gown bothered her or not. This woman was so different from any he'd ever met.

"It's nice."

She didn't answer, and he didn't know what else to say. So

he said nothing, as nighttime noises soon took over. Crickets. A Whippoorwill. Each sound more calming than the last.

"Are you worried about the fence, Monty?" Her soft voice barely broke through the nocturnal noises.

Was his concern that easy to read? He'd not intended to undermine Jacob in front of the others. He should correct that lapse. Now. With Grace. But he couldn't quite bring himself to lie to her. "Jacob said the demonstration was impressive."

He could feel her gaze on him, but he kept his focus toward the darkness.

"Are you worried about it?" The same question. She wasn't going to let him side-step.

At last, he let the spent air leak from him in a long breath. "I don't know how I feel. Jacob's opinions are usually solid. But something about it makes me uneasy. I can't put my finger on it, so... Maybe it's nothing."

"Have you talked to him about your concern?"

He glanced at her. A single ray of moonlight lit part of her face, revealing only one of her shining eyes. "No. I don't have anything specific to tell him. Just a gut feeling." He turned back toward the shadows. How could he put into words the uneasiness? It wouldn't make enough sense to carry weight in a discussion. Why was he even telling her?

"Seems to me he'd value the wisdom in your opinion. I know I would."

Monty glanced back at her, but she didn't meet his gaze, just stared ahead.

Then, before he could react, she turned with a quiet swish. "I'll leave you be. Sorry to bother." And she was gone, before he could stop her.

Silence descended over him again, but it wasn't the same as before. This time, the emptiness of it all tightened his chest. How could one slender lady take all the peacefulness with her?

The squeak of the door sounded again, and relief flooded

over Monty in a wave stronger than it should have. She'd come back. But as he turned to greet her, the words died on his tongue.

Bo's form outlined against the light through the doorway, as his boots thudded on the porch. "Thought I might find you out here. Escaping."

Monty bit back a retort and turned to stare into the darkness again. "Not escaping. Just enjoying the quiet."

Bo was kind enough not to answer that, but he didn't keep quiet long. "I guess we're headed back tomorrow. It's been a good trip."

Monty turned to him. "Already? I thought you might stay 'til the weekend at least."

His brother shook his head. "Miranda's not feeling so good again, and I need to get back to the ranch."

Monty raised a hand to clasp Bo's shoulder. "It's been good to see you. You've got a great family, Bo. You should be proud of them."

Bo's white teeth flashed in the darkness. "I am. Looks like you're not far from your own family either."

Monty almost choked on the breath he'd been inhaling. "What are you talking about?"

Bo shifted into the shaft of moonlight so Monty could see his raised brows. "Grace seems like quite a catch."

Swallowing, Monty turned away so Bo wouldn't see any emotion in his eyes. "She's just a hired hand. Not even one I hired. Did I tell you Anna brought her on?"

"Doesn't mean you haven't settled into the idea of having her around."

Monty issued a snort to disguise his discomfort. Was he that obvious? First his unease about the wire fencing, now this. He needed to get a better handle on his emotions.

"Monty." Bo's voice lost any hint of teasing. "I'm only going to say this once. Then later I'll say I told you so. But I see how you look at Grace. If you don't snatch her up, somebody else will. And you know exactly what that feels like. I've never seen you look at any of those other women like you do this one every time she walks into the room. You better make your move. And make it quick."

Monty's pulse kicked up a notch. Did they have to talk about this now? The way he felt about Grace was such a jumble in his mind. She was his employee, for goodness sake. It wasn't right for him to take advantage or think of her in any other way.

"Well." Bo slapped him on the back. "I'll let you get back to enjoying the quiet."

As the click of boot leather on wood retreated into the house, Monty dropped his head into his hands. What should he do? Part of him wanted to find excuses to be near Grace. And the other part told him he needed a good dousing in the water trough to get his head straightened out.

Lord, which prompting is from you?

CHAPTER 9

The next two weeks passed in a blur, with calving season in full swing. Grace had already assisted with more than two dozen births, and it never ceased to amaze her as she watched the dawn of a new life. Especially when all went well during the delivery.

Unfortunately, even though the longhorns were a sturdy lot, not every calving was smooth. Like the one she and Santiago just attended. The baby was breeched and the mama had pushed for a while before Grace found her. They'd finally got the little one moved back from the birthing canal and turned around, but by the time the birth finished, the mother was too weak to survive. Part of her insides had come out with the calf, and there was nothing to do but put her out of her misery. A sad loss of life.

But at least the calf lived—a little heifer, now laying across Grace's saddle. They'd managed to get some of the mother's milk into the baby right away, but now the little tike was officially a foundling. She'd join the other two orphan calves at the barn, another mouth for Juan or Chester to feed after each milking.

"You're a strong one though, aren't you?" Grace stroked the calf's neck.

It raised its head from her leg and let out a sad bleat.

"I know. You miss your mama, but Mr. Juan's gonna take good care of you." She reined Georgina to a stop in front of the barn. No movement stirred around the building. "Juan? Chester?"

Seconds later, a head of dark hair and a freckled face appeared through the crack in the barn door. "Miss Grace." Chester jogged out.

"I brought you a new friend. Can you help me get her down?"

"Yes'm."

"You get her front." Grace leaned forward and slid her leg over the horse's rump while still supporting the calf's back end.

It emitted a rather frantic moo and scrambled as Grace and Chester lowered it to the ground.

"It's all right, little girl. I'll take you in to see your friends." Chester stroked the calf's glossy tan hide as he spoke.

"Where's Juan? She's had a little bit of milk, but needs more soon. She's about two hours old."

Chester looked up at Grace. "Juan was feeling poorly so he went to take a catnap. I'll get her settled and feed her a bit. Don't worry, Miss Grace."

She watched them shuffle into the barn, Chester bent low as he guided the calf with both hands. He was a good lad, but bucket feeding a calf could be tricky the first few times until the animal got the hang of it. The task was certainly easier with two people.

Turning back to Georgina, she pulled the mare's reins over her head. "Let's get you tied, girl. I think we're going to hang around a few minutes to help."

It turned out the calf took quite readily to drinking from the bucket. It was a feisty thing, and kept butting the bottom of the pail with its nose, but Chester held the handle steady.

Grace stepped back to the stall rail to watch. "You said Juan's not feeling well? Does he need a doctor?"

Chester gave her a sideways glance. "I've been tellin' him to go see the doc in town, but he says it's jest old age. Most days he gets awful winded after we finish ridin' the colts."

Grace mulled the words in her mind. "Juan doesn't still break the young ones, does he?" Had he looked frail the last few times she'd seen him? She couldn't say for sure.

"No, ma'am. I do most of the ridin'. Juan tells me what to do, and he gets on 'em ever so often."

Still...

The jingle of a wagon and a horse's whinny sounded from outside. Chester's head popped up, but Grace raised a staying hand. "You finish that. I'll see who it is."

Had Mr. O'Brien gone to town today? She didn't remember hearing about a trip, but then again, she was just a hired hand. Not privy to all the family's comings and goings.

As she stepped through the barn door, an unfamiliar wagon reined to a stop in front of her. A dark-haired man with a full, curly beard climbed down.

"Can I help you, sir?"

He scanned her, starting with her face all the way down to her boots, then back up again. She'd experienced the same kind of perusal more than once, but she still had to fight to keep the heat from climbing to her face.

"What can I help you with, sir?" She spoke a little louder this time, and took a half step forward.

He settled back on his heels and propped a fist on his hip. "We-ell." He drawled out the word. "I'm lookin' fer the man of the place. Got a wagon load o' wire here fer 'im."

The wire. Grace glanced in the wagon where a row of crates lined the far side. "All right. Wait here and I'll go get him."

She turned on her heel, more than a little relieved to be leaving the man's hawk-eyed appraisal. But the burn of his stare followed her across the yard to the house. All had been quiet inside when she'd gone in for the milk earlier. It was about the right time for the children to take naps, so maybe she'd find Mr. O'Brien in his office.

Stepping inside, she tried not to cringe at the loud click of her boots on the wooden floor. "Hello? Mr. O'Brien?" The office door was open, but all chairs proved vacant. The parlor? She checked the room but it was empty, too. A door opened down the hall and Grace spun.

"Grace?"

"Anna. The man's here to deliver the fence wire. Is Mr. O'Brien around?"

Anna scrunched her nose. "No. He had business in Seguin, but he said he already paid for the shipment in full. Can you ask Juan and Chester to help him unload, and I'll be out in a few minutes to sign for it? I need to stay in here until I'm sure Martin's asleep."

"Of course." Grace retraced her steps out to the wagon.

The driver had an elbow cocked against one side, deep in conversation with Chester. Or rather, answering each of the questions the boy peppered at him. The man seemed content to prattle on, and didn't shift his position as Grace rounded the wagon to join them.

"...then I met Mr. Glidden an' he needed someone to tote this wire 'round the country. Suits me jest fine."

Grace cleared her throat. "Sir. We're to begin unloading the supplies. Mrs. O'Brien will be out directly to sign for the shipment."

The man turned to her with another all-encompassing look. "Ain't got no menfolk 'round here?"

She held the man's stare, but out of the corner of her eye, she saw Chester stiffen. "Of course. Chester and I will help you unload. Please back your wagon into the barn to shorten the carrying distance." Without waiting for his response, she spun and strode toward the barn to swing wide the massive doors.

By the time the man backed the wagon inside, she had a spot cleared out near the remnants of stored hay. She hoped in spades Monty would want the wire stacked in the barn, otherwise they'd have their hands full hauling all those crates to the new location. Eyeing them now, there looked to be about twenty cases loaded in the wagon.

As the driver dismounted, Chester grabbed the first box and grunted as he pulled it from the bed. Grace reached for the next in line.

She almost dropped the thing on her toe as it strained every muscle in her back and shoulders. What was in these crates, solid steel? She clamped her jaw and focused her muscles as she shuffled toward the area Chester had placed his. She would not prove weaker than a boy and a man who spent his days perched on a wagon seat.

But by the time she carried her fifth box toward the row in the hay, she was ready to accede her weakness. Every muscle she possessed had been screaming for a while now, and most had turned to mush. Who knew she was such a weakling?

By the time Chester carried the last crate, even he looked to be tiring.

Graced forced her shoulders back as she addressed the driver. "You can pull your rig from the barn. I'll let Mrs. O'Brien know you're ready."

She dragged herself into the house and found Anna rocking baby Martin in the parlor.

The young mother gave her an apologetic look. "I'm sorry, Grace. He just won't give in to sleep. Are the men finished unloading?"

Grace smiled past the question. "Everything's unloaded. The driver just needs the delivery papers signed." The last thing she wanted was to get Juan in trouble when he wasn't feeling well. She stepped closer. "Would you like me to sit with the babe while you go outside?"

"Oh, would you? That'd be a blessing. Thank you, dear." Anna handed over the bundled baby, and he immediately started squirming to sit up.

"Easy, fella. Let's see if we can get you sleepy." Grace crooned to the child as she shuffled over to sit in the rocker. Her legs almost buckled when she sank into the chair. Yes, a chance to sit and rock was exactly what her tired muscles needed.

~

Grace didn't make it back out to the cattle that afternoon.

By the time Anna returned to the house and she'd handed off the sleeping Martin, Chester asked for her help moving a small herd of horses from one corral to the other. After checking on the calves one more time, she headed out to where she'd tied Georgina.

But a line of cowboys showed on the horizon, riding from the direction of the main herd. The rest of the cowpunchers coming in for the day.

"Well. I guess we're all done, girl." She rubbed her mare's face as she watched Monty's strong outline leading the riders toward the barn. Shifting toward the saddle, she unfastened the girth, but kept up her murmuring to the horse. "Sorry you had to stand tied out here."

When Monty drew near, she stepped away from the mare to meet him. "Sorry I didn't make it back out there. The delivery of fence wire came, and I was needed to help unload."

His mouth pinched. "Not a problem. Just glad everything's all right." His face had that stoic look that was so hard to read.

Was he angry? Did he think she was shirking her duties? Or maybe it was concern over the arrival of the dreaded fence.

Nothing she could do about it now. Turning away, Grace trudged back to her work.

~

Hank Thornhill shifted his weight on the wagon's bench as the outskirts of San Antonio loomed ahead. Sure would be nice to hit a decent saloon, maybe see that pretty blonde who'd been makin' eyes at him last time he came through. Sure as shootin', that little town of Seguin didn't have nothin' on the fun in San Antone.

Of course, the delivery yesterday to the ranch where with that gal in britches had been a bit of pleasure. Pretty little thing. Somethin' about her had seemed so familiar, but he still couldn't quite put his thumb on it. It t'weren't every day a man got ta see a gal dressed up like a feller. The clothes sure didn't cover up those curves, though.

He reined in the horses at the livery and jumped from the wagon. "Just need 'em bedded down fer the night, Jack. I'll be headed out early."

"Got it." The livery owner took hold of the lead horse's bridle, leaving Hank free to enjoy the night.

Grabbing his bedroll from the back of the wagon, he strolled in the direction of the red light district. As he passed the Post Office, he slowed to take a gander at the posters in the window. His eye caught one near the bottom, with a sketch of a woman's face.

He froze.

By jingo, it was her. The same shape to her face, same look in the eye. Purty as all git out. Even showed her hair braided just like it'd been yesterday.

He squinted at the words beneath the picture.

Missing. Grace Hampstead, brown hair, blue eyes, aged twenty-eight. $1000 for information which helps discover her location. Contact Leonard Fulton, Santa Ana, California.

A thousand dollars? Saints and angels, he wouldn't have to work again for years. Maybe never, if this luck hung on long enough for him ta git in a few games of poker.

He tried the Post Office door, but it was already locked for the day. Blast. This was the only place in town to send a telegram, too. Well, he'd be jiggered if he weren't standin' here on the stoop the minute it opened tomorrow morning.

No sense in keepin' this Leonard Fulton fella waitin'.

CHAPTER 10

Monty studied the roll of wire on the ground in front of him, then eyed the tree line marking the northern edge of Double Rocking B property. How exactly had Jacob figured to mount the stuff? It didn't come with any kind of sketch or instructions, just a roll of double sided barbs that left his hand bloody after only pulling it from the crate.

Jacob had planned to be out helping this first day, but he'd felt poorly that morning and had looked pale as a sheet. It hadn't taken much to convince him to stay home. Not usual for his resilient friend, but every man had his limits.

So now, it was up to Monty to find the best way to build the fence. The property line ended at the edge of the woods so they could use trees as fence posts. Should the wire be wrapped around the trees? That seemed like a waste of the stuff when some of these trunks were two or three foot thick.

He glanced up at Nathan. The man stood quietly, waiting for Monty's command. "I think this might work best if we nailed it up. Last I saw, we had a bucket of nails in the storage room on the back of the barn. Reckon' you could ride back and get 'em?"

"Sure, boss."

Monty pulled his hands from his pockets and winced as the scratches caught on the wool trouser cloth. He turned to Nathan. "Bring some good thick gloves, too. Several pairs."

With the help of Jesse and Santiago, they had the wire unraveled and laid out along the tree line by the time Nathan returned. The nails proved to be just the thing, especially when they tapped them into the tree a half inch, then bent them over to snug the wire in place.

After they'd secured the wire to three trees, Monty stepped back and eyed their work. "I think we're going to have to pull it tighter, boys." From being wound in rings inside the crate, the wire had developed kinks and coils and had a definite sway to it between the trees. Would that really hold in the livestock? They'd have to run a second strand for sure. This one was mounted at eye level to a full grown cow, but another wire would need to be hung a couple feet below it to keep in the younger animals.

By the time the sun hit the center of the noon sky, they'd made it halfway through the wire from the first crate. It had been slow going at first, but they were getting the hang of it now, with three men pulling the wire tight while the fourth nailed it to the tree. Of course, all four of them had cuts and gashes all the way up their arms from those wicked barbs.

One thing was for sure, this was a man's job. He'd not be putting Grace through the rotation onto the fence-building crew. It was bad enough she pulled a man's weight with the cattle.

~

race nibbled at her cinnamon roll as dinner conversation flowed around her. The men from the fence crew were chock-full of stories about how hard the wire was to hang. And with Luis among them, it seemed there'd been no shortage of pranks on the job either.

Over the past week and a half, the crew had been rotating a new man out each day, so her turn should come soon. In fact, now that she thought about it, she was the only hand that hadn't been assigned fence duty. Not that she was eager, but…she was curious.

Would the wire really keep the cattle from barging right through? They'd been pasturing the herd in the southeast section of the ranch, closest to the Guadalupe, so she'd not even seen the work done on the north side yet.

Monty's chair scraped as he pushed back from the table. An expectant hush fell over the room. "Nathan, you can take Jesse's place with the fence tomorrow."

"Yes, sir."

And then the flurry of motion and noise commenced as the men stood and filed toward the door.

Nathan? But he'd already worked his four days on the fence crew. Did that mean…? Grace bit her tongue, but she could feel the muscles across her forehead pulling tight.

She waited in the hallway as Monty spoke a few words to Mr. O'Brien, then fell into step behind the last of the men. As he passed her, he tipped his chin, but didn't let his gaze meet hers. "G'night, Grace."

"Monty?"

He paused and turned, still not quite looking her in the eyes.

"Can I have a word?"

He glanced toward the men slipping through the front door, then back at her. "Sure. You wanna go in the parlor or out on the porch?"

"The porch is fine." Their voices would probably carry from the parlor, and the family didn't need to hear her frustrations. Besides, the fresh night air would be a welcome relief.

He strode to the front door, then held it and motioned for her to precede him.

Grace stepped outside, inhaled a steadying breath, then turned on him. "I'm not sure if you're aware, but I haven't helped with the fence crew yet."

"Really." The word didn't sound like a question, more like a patronizing statement.

She narrowed her eyes, but they'd not brought a lantern, and his face was shadowed in the darkness. He probably couldn't see her either. "Really. Are you not planning for me to carry my load like the rest of the men?"

He was quiet for a long moment. Had he really forgotten her in the rotation? It wasn't possible. So what was his objection? She'd just opened her mouth to ask him when he finally spoke.

"Grace." His voice sounded so…resigned. No, almost pained.

"What is it, Monty?" She reached forward and touched his arm before she could stop herself. But she didn't pull back. Not at first. Not until his chin dropped and she could feel the weight of his stare on her hand, even in the darkness.

Her muscles tensed to withdraw her reach, but before she could, the warmth of his hand settled over hers. He held her secure within his grasp, the heat of him sending tingles all the way up her arm. She wanted nothing more than to turn her wrist and entwine her fingers in his. Or maybe step closer, as his warmth seemed to draw her.

"Grace, I…" He stopped, and she barely breathed as she waited for him to speak again. What had they been discussing? It didn't matter. If only she could see the expression in his dark, chocolate eyes.

With the slightest of squeezes, he removed his hand and stepped back, pulling his arm from her reach.

Her hand dropped to her side. Limp.

"Grace. I'm not planning to put you on the fence crew. I'd

rather have you with the cattle." And with that parting shot, he turned and strode down the stairs.

She stood rooted to the porch, trying desperately to force her thoughts into some semblance of order. She'd been so befuddled by his touch, she'd not even argued her case. Even now, there was no fight left in her.

Had he done that intentionally? Surely not. Surely he hadn't missed the connection in their touch. Because her whole body still tingled from it. The warmth of his hand still pulsed through her arm. What was she supposed to do with that?

~

Monty lay in his bunk, eyes wide open as the vigorous strains of a fiddle drifted through the air. This was no languid ballad like the last time Grace played. This one had spirit, as if she were venting fiery emotions through the instrument's strings. If she was in half as much turmoil over their touch as he was, she'd be playing for hours.

What had he been thinking, holding her hand like that? But when she'd reached out, he'd not been able to stop himself. Well, actually he'd done a pretty decent job of stopping himself—from taking her in his arms and tasting those full lips.

Lord, what am I thinking? He scrubbed a hand down his face. He had to make a decision where Grace was concerned. 'Cause having her on his staff—so close every single day—and treating her like any of the others was driving him loco. *Muy loco.*

But what were the other options? Send her away? Marry her? He'd known the woman less than two months. How on earth could he make that kind of decision in such a short amount of time?

If you don't snatch her up, somebody else will. Bo's words drifted back to haunt him. He bit back a groan and rolled onto his side. He wasn't making a decision until God made the way clear.

Now if he could just make his mind and body remember that.

~

"Easy, girl. Time to slow down for the night." Grace gave the reins a gentle tug as the mare beneath her picked up speed. The ranch buildings were in sight, but the horse had put in a hard day's work and needed to cool her muscles so she didn't stove up in the corral tonight.

The line of cowpunchers had spread out as they'd trekked in from the pastures, some horses dragging more than others.

Santiago rode just in front of her. He glanced back, then reined his horse until he was beside her. "Weather sure has been nice these days."

She glanced around at the bluebonnets just starting to bloom. "Yes, your Texas springs are pretty. Once you get past the rain anyway."

Santiago cleared his throat. But then he didn't say anything.

Grace turned to look at him. Sweat glistened on the man's forehead, with a bead of it running down his temple. Was he ill? "Santiago, is everything all right?"

He cleared his throat again. "I, uh, was wondering if you have any plans after church tomorrow? I mean..." Again, his throat cleared, this time sounding a bit like a strangled calf. "If you don't have anything else to do, would you like to go on a picnic? By the river. With me."

Mercy. The last thing she wanted was to encourage romantic attention from him or any other man here. Except maybe Monty. No, not even Monty.

But as she glanced at the man beside her and tried her best to come up with a way to politely decline, she lost her nerve. His face was almost as white as when he'd been bitten by the rattler, and his eyes had that wide, scared look, like a jackrabbit about to dart into the bushes.

She forced a gentle smile. "That would be nice. I can put together a basket of food if you'd like."

The smile that bloomed on his face bordered on ridiculous, but it certainly sent warmth through her chest. He'd been a good friend these last couple months. The least she could do was share a meal with him.

~

Monty eyed the handful of cowpunchers scattered around the table for Sunday lunch. It was typical for some of the men to skip the meal. He'd always given them freedom on their day off, except for church, of course.

But where was Grace? She'd never been absent before. Was she sick?

He glanced toward Jacob at the other end of the table, busy in a murmured conversation with his wife. His gaze wandered around the table. Santiago might know where she was. The two of them seemed to be decent friends since he'd paired them up when Grace first arrived. But Santiago looked to be absent, too.

Monty turned to Donato, who caught his gaze with a strange expression. Should he ask his cousin? Later. When they weren't in front of a crowd.

But as he tried to follow Donato from the dining room, Jacob stopped Monty to talk about progress on the fence. By the time he stepped outside, Donato had disappeared. Not in the bunkhouse, not in the barn. He finally found him behind the house, perched on the stoop at the kitchen door and whittling a tiny piece of wood.

Monty settled onto the step beside him. "Watcha making?"

"Toy animals for the little master. They take me long enough, I might have the set done before he's too old to play with them." He held up the rough shape of an animal. A horse maybe. Or a donkey. For that matter it could be a cow. "You ever think about settling down, Monty? Having niños of your own?"

Monty cut his cousin a sideways glance. Donato focused on his knife as it scraped across the figurine's back. Was he asking for more than general conversation?

"Maybe." Only every other day for about fifteen years now. But he'd long since resigned himself to life as a bachelor. And he enjoyed running the ranch here. Working with his cousins and the others who were practically family. It took away the ache for a woman of his own. Most days.

He tightened his jaw. Those weren't the thoughts he'd come out here to drudge up. "You know where Grace is this afternoon? Is she sick? It's not like her to skip meals."

Donato gave him a quick sideways glance, and a smile played at the corners of his mouth as he went back to studying the wood. "The way I heard it, she didn't skip the meal. Santiago took her on a picnic by the river."

Monty choked on the breath he'd just inhaled. "What?" Flashes of white flickered on the edge of his vision, as a weightless feeling washed through his head.

Donato shrugged. "Sounds like he's got more brains than the rest of us. Not sayin' I hadn't thought about it myself, just hadn't worked up the nerve yet."

The weightlessness disappeared as blood pumped through Monty. Faster, harder. He could almost hear the thump in his chest. "And she agreed to it?"

Another shrug.

Vaulting to his feet, Monty paced several steps and spun. "Why didn't you stop them?"

Donato raised a single brow. "Why would I do that? There's no law against courting a grown woman. At least, not that I know of."

"*Why?*" It took every ounce of his effort not to march over and yank Donato up by his shirt front. "Because he can't... She can't..." Oh, he wanted to holler. He had to get out of there before he did something really dumb.

Spinning on his heel, Monty strode for the barn.

"Monty." Donato's sharp command slowed Monty's step only a little. "*Don't* ride out there."

His feet halted, but he didn't turn around. Had he been planning to ride to the river? To break up their little outing? Dropping his head, he pressed his fingers into his temples. What was he doing?

Slowly, he turned to the right. North. Opposite from the direction of the river.

And he started walking. Past the bunkhouse, out into the fields, through the woods and all the way to Oklahoma if that's what it took. He wouldn't stop until he'd made a decision.

CHAPTER 11

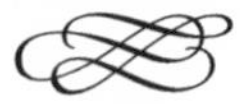

Monty's breath came in deep lungfuls by the time his heartbeat finally settled to a tolerable speed. The row of barbed wire fence stood sentry not far ahead. He might really end up in Oklahoma at this point. But the fire was mostly gone from his veins now and had left behind a deep disturbance in his spirit.

He crouched down to sit on a log beside the trail, then pulled off his hat and tossed it to the ground. Bowing his head, he dragged in a deep inhale, stilling some of the turmoil in his mind.

After holding that posture for several moments, he tried to pray. "Lord."

But no words came. *God, I need help here*. The cry came from deep within him, but it brought with it a measure of peace.

He stayed that way. Just…being. After a few moments, one of the verses from Psalms the pastor read that morning came back to him. *Oh that men would praise the Lord for His goodness, and for His wonderful works to the children of men! For He satisfieth the longing soul, and filleth the hungry soul with goodness.*

Longing soul. If that didn't perfectly describe him, there

weren't any words that could. But what was it he craved so much? *God setteth the solitary in families: he bringeth out those which are bound with chains.* The verse flittered through his mind like a breeze.

Is that what had built up this powerful unrest? He scrubbed a hand through his hair. "God, I've been asking for a wife for years now. I just haven't understood why You kept saying no." To tell the truth, it'd been hard to forgive the Almighty each time he'd dangled a woman in front of Monty, then married her off to someone else. There were a few times it took a good long talk with the Lord to come to terms with whatever His master plan was.

"So what, God? What do you want from me now?" As much as he'd been trying to build a wall against her, Grace's image took hold in his mind. Was this God's special form of torture? Trying to teach him self-control?

"What do You want from me?" His words came louder this time, and he pressed fingers into his eye sockets to try to wipe away the images in his mind. "I know I can't have her."

Why not? The words were so real, he raised his head and looked around for the source.

Why not? Because she was his hired hand. Because he'd only known her a couple months. Because...

Because God had never said yes to a woman in his life before, how could he fathom Grace might be the answer this time?

Monty dropped his head and let it hang. Was that what this all boiled down to? God had been trying to hand him a blessing on a silver platter, but he'd been fighting it like a calf at branding? Surely he wasn't that thickheaded.

"God, if you brought Grace for me, I'm gonna need You to give me a clear sign here. This is too big to mess up."

A picture of Grace and Santiago sitting by the river formed in his mind. Not what he wanted to think about right now. Did she have feelings for the man? Would he be setting himself up for more heartbreak if he pursued her?

Bo's words came to him again. *If you don't snatch her up, somebody else will. You better make your move quick.*

Purpose flooded his chest, beating through his veins with every pump of blood. Yes, if God was blessing him with a woman—this woman—he was done being dull-witted. It was time to woo her.

And his first step would be to stake his claim. No more picnics with Santiago. She was spoken for.

But it was a good thing Monty had the entire walk back to the ranch to think through his strategy. Showing up at the riverside to interrupt the picnic was probably not the best approach to win Grace's heart. Although it'd work pretty well to embarrass her if that was his aim.

Nope. He needed to find a quiet time to talk with her. But should he come right out and say he wanted to marry her? Or be subtle and try to woo her? Women liked that sort of thing, didn't they?

But how in the state of Texas was he supposed to do that? Certainly not while they worked with the cattle. He'd never live it down with the other men. And that wasn't the way the boss should behave anyway. He'd have to find time in the evenings and on Sundays. And here he'd wasted almost the whole Sabbath already.

Maybe she'd be open to a walk after dinner tonight. His hands grew sweaty just thinking about it. Maybe he wasn't quite ready for this courting thing. But he didn't have time to waste. He'd have to push through his nerves like he pushed through the other obstacles in his life.

And the more he thought about it, the more having Grace in his life would be worth the effort.

~

For having spent the day in *rest,* Grace was exhausted. She forced another bite of stew to her mouth. She wasn't even that hungry after the late lunch with Santiago, and her head pounded at her temples.

They'd had a nice time by the river. The view certainly made the trip worthwhile, with all the blooming bluebonnets and cherry trees. Spring in Texas was a sight to behold.

But it had been a lot of work to keep the conversation going for several hours. The times she'd allowed it to lapse had grown quickly into uncomfortable silence, bringing back all those memories of social visits Mama would drag her on at nearby ranches.

The sound of chairs scraping forced her attention up. The handful of cowpunchers who'd joined the evening meal were all shuffling toward the door.

She rose and fell into step behind Donato. She could already imagine the softness of her feather mattress and the cotton bed linens. Almost nothing stood between her and their warm comfort now. As soon as she made it up the stairs.

Gripping the bannister, she pulled herself up one step at a time, the pounding in her head ricocheting with each effort.

"Grace?"

She'd only made it to the fourth stair when Monty's voice stopped her. Keeping her neck straight to minimize the pulsing, she eased around to face him. "Yes?"

"I was wondering if you'd like to take a walk. The weather's nice out tonight."

Walk? No, she wanted to collapse into soft oblivion. But she forced her mouth into something that might pass for a smile. "Is there something specific you wanted to discuss?"

He glanced down at his boots as they scuffed against the wooden floor. When he looked back up, he didn't quite meet her gaze. "Nothing special. Just thought it might be nice to get out."

A part of her wanted to say yes. Craved the chance to spend undivided time with him. But the throbbing working its way up her neck and pulsing through her skull kept her from agreeing. She wouldn't be fit company. "I'd like to, Monty. But I'm not feeling very well tonight. I think I'd better go to bed."

He studied her for a moment, then looked away. "Get some rest. Hope you feel better in the morning."

She watched him turn and stride back toward the dining room. Something in her stomach tightened as he disappeared through the open doorway. She should have said yes. Should have jumped at the chance. But it was lost to her now.

Turning back to the stairs, she pulled herself up to the next step. Everything would be better after sleep.

She was just slipping her hands through the sleeves on her night dress when a soft knock sounded on her door. "Just a minute." Pulling the worn cotton cloth down quickly, she grabbed her wrapper and padded to the door. "Who's there?"

"It's Anna."

Grace pulled the door open a crack, enough to see Anna on the threshold, a worry line creasing her brow. She opened it wider. "Come in. Can I help with something?"

Anna slipped inside. "Monty said you were ill. Wanted me to come check on you." She reached a hand to Grace's forehead. "Are you feverish? You do look pale."

Grace closed her eyes to soak in the human contact. How long had it been since someone had touched her, even in such a simple gesture? Not since Monty placed his hand atop hers those weeks ago. The memory of that sent a warmth through her chest. She forced it aside. "I'm all right. Just a headache. Nothing a good night's sleep won't cure."

Anna eyed her with a dubious expression. "Are you sure? Monty's downstairs pacing a hole in my floor, he's so worried about you. He took the baby from my arms and sent me straight up here."

Grace fought to keep her jaw from dropping. "He did? I didn't mean to worry him. It really is just a headache. He asked me on a walk, but I knew I wouldn't be fit company tonight."

The doubtful expression cleared from Anna's face, replaced by raised brows. "Monty asked you to walk with him? Under the stars?"

She glanced toward the window, but couldn't see anything besides the black of night. "I don't know if there are stars out. I hope I didn't upset him by saying no, I just..." A wave of exhaustion washed over her, culminating in a yawn too strong to hold back.

Anna stroked her shoulder. "Go to bed. Poor thing, you've been working too hard lately. I'll tell Monty not to worry."

Grace forced a smile. "Thank you."

After Anna left, she moved to the wash basin and splashed water on her face. With the towel pressed against her eyes, she thought through Anna's words. Monty had been so worried he'd sent the woman up to check on her. Was that normal for a boss? It seemed out of character for solid, stoic Monty. Could it possibly mean he...cared for her? That couldn't be true, yet her skin still tingled with the memory of his touch. Had he felt the same?

But the bigger question—did she want him to? If Leonard found her trail and followed her here, she'd have no choice but to run. Monty could only be a memory at that point. She had to do her best to make sure it wasn't a painful one.

For either of them.

~

The rumble of thunder reverberated in the distance as the cattle pushed through the trail opening into the pasture ahead. Grace reined Pepper to the left to cut off several yearling cows trying to make an escape through the woods. "Get on, heifers. The grass is straight ahead."

Just when she had them headed back to the herd, a spear of lightning lit the evening sky, followed by another loud crack. One of the cows darted sideways.

The coming storm had all the animals squirrelly as jackrabbits. Even Pepper's nerves were on edge as the mare wheeled sideways to catch the rogue cow. She was turning into a decent cow horse, although still not quite as solid as Georgina.

When they finally had the herd in the pasture, with all the stragglers out of the trees, Grace joined the cluster of cowboys by the trail head.

Monty raised his hat, swiped a sleeve across his forehead, then positioned the brim back in place. "I reckon' they're as settled as they're gonna be until the storm passes. We can head in for the night."

The group turned back to the trail through the woods, and rode in pairs to fit the width of the path. Grace glanced at Monty beside her. "You had a good idea to split the herd into smaller groups with the storm coming."

He nodded. "Too many cattle in one spot makes a higher chance of stampede. I learned that lesson one too many times."

She glanced at him with a raised brow. "Anything happen recently?"

"Not for several years. But there was one year we lost a third of our spring calves during a summer storm. Haven't had a problem with it since we started splitting the herds into less than five hundred each."

After a moment, he asked, "Did you have many stampedes with your father's cattle?"

She thought back through the years. "One or two that I can remember. We didn't get near as much rain as you do here, so the storms were mostly dry lightning. Mama never let me help during a stampede, though." She cringed the moment the words left her mouth. She sounded like an adolescent school girl whose mother wouldn't let her soil her shoes. "I was young at the time. We haven't had a stampede for at least the last dozen years."

They rode in silence for a while until the trail left the woods and opened into a different pasture, where another small herd of cattle grazed. Monty motioned to the cowpunchers circling the cattle and waved them toward the direction of home.

Lightning flashed again, followed closely by a crack of thunder. Monty looked back at the herd behind them and Grace followed his gaze. The cattle milled about, lowing occasionally in protest of the coming storm. Definitely not grazing quietly anymore.

"Do you think they'll be all right?"

He took so long to answer, she wasn't sure he heard. At last he sighed. "I hope so. I don't want to keep the boys out in this storm, though. Not much I could do if I stay by myself. We'll hear 'em if they start to run."

Grace nibbled her lower lip. She wouldn't mind staying to help. But the two of them would be close to helpless if the herd decided to stampede.

Still… "I'll stay out here, Monty, if you think it would help."

He cut her a glance. But as he opened his mouth to answer, another crash rent the air, flooding the stormy sky with light and thunderous sound.

As the light died away, the rumble of thunder reverberated, growing in volume with each second. Grace spun her horse along with the rest of the men, an icy dread filling her chest.

A stampede.

CHAPTER 12

The sight of the massive herd galloping—gathering momentum like water over a fall—was enough to freeze any sane person. Their power would have been magnificent if it weren't so deadly.

She plunged her heels into Pepper's sides, spurring the mare into a hard run. Wired as the horse was from the storm and the roar of thousands of hooves, it took her only seconds to stretch into long, ground-covering strides. With a shaky hand, Grace reached for the revolver at her hip.

The men all raced the same direction. If someone could get to the front of the herd and fire some shots, they had a chance to slow the out-of-control longhorns.

They had to.

If this group made it to the next pasture where another herd grazed, the size of the stampede would double. And with it, the number of animals lost.

As the surging mass neared the pass between two sections of trees, Grace pushed her mare harder. The front of the pack was less than thirty feet ahead of her. If she could just gain more ground…

A shot split the air. Wild cries from cattle almost deafened.

More gunfire. The frantic whinny of a horse.

Shouts from the men.

And then the roar of hooves died away.

Grace reined Pepper down to a walk as she approached the front of the herd, the animals now milling in frantic circles.

"Spread out around them." Monty's voice rose above the bellows of the cattle.

Grace glanced at the positions of the other men. Dusk was taking over quickly, and she had to squint to see the far side of the herd. Keeping Pepper at a walk so as not to upset the longhorns any more, she circled to the right.

The rain came less than a quarter hour later, but it seemed to chase the lightning away. For another quarter hour, they could see quick bursts of light in the distance, far enough away the thunder simmered in a low rumble.

She'd never been so happy to be wet, guarding her post in the torrent of rain while the cattle braced themselves against the pelting drops.

Monty rode by a few minutes later. "Gonna check the stampede path. See if there's any animals we can save."

"Shall I come help?" She called loud enough to be heard over the din.

He didn't look back, but waved her forward.

As she neared the rear of the herd, spots of dark littered the ground through the torrential downpour. Monty was already crouched next to one form. Grace reined Pepper at another and slid to the ground.

A brown and white spotted calf. The unnatural position of its neck told a quick tale of its fate. She turned away, moving on to the next figure.

This one was alive, but just barely. Hoof marks marred the wet hair along its abdomen. Most likely a lung had been crushed in the trample of the stampede. These poor calves just weren't big enough or strong enough to keep up with the herd in full distress.

And so it went, calf after calf. Somewhere along the way, Grace's tears began to mingle with the rain on her cheeks. So much destruction. So many innocent little lives.

She knelt beside a black calf, this one still moving. It looked to be several months old, and tried to raise its head. "Hey there." She stroked the wet neck. "What's wrong with you?"

The calf struggled again and finally sat up. She rubbed its neck, then ran her hands over the angular body. Nothing she could see looked broken. Both nostrils flared with steady breathing. Was there a chance this one might be all right? Maybe she'd just been stunned by a blow to the head.

She rubbed the calf's body in a circular motion, forcing life-restoring blood to pump through all its limbs. After a few moments of this, the calf extended a hoof, then tried to push up to its feet.

"Thatta girl." Grace moved behind the animal to help push it up.

The front legs seemed to work, but the rear legs just wouldn't unfold. The calf sank back to the ground, but the flame of hope grew brighter in Grace. "You almost did it, sweet one. Let's try again."

She scrubbed the calf's hindquarters, and it positioned its front feet for another try. This time, the back legs worked a little better, although they struggled to hold the weight of the animal. Grace braced it on both sides to help balance. "You did it."

Little by little, she loosened her hold until the calf stood by its own strength. She kept a hand on its neck, stroking. "I think you're gonna make it, girl. What say we get you to your mama? Think you can walk?"

With gentle proddings, the animal took a few shaky baby steps, just like a newborn. This girl must have been knocked completely senseless. After several strides, its gait became steady and picked up speed, although it still allowed Grace to guide with one hand on the rump and another at the chest.

When they reached the herd, the calf let out a loud bawl. Several cows answered, but one call rose above the rest. Grace straightened and smiled as the calf trotted forward to meet its eager mother.

While she watched the pair through the near darkness, a touch settled on her shoulder. She tensed and glanced up, her muscles preparing to flee.

But Monty's kind eyes met her gaze, and she relaxed into them. He looked at the calf, and Grace turned back to follow his gaze.

"You did good with her." His voice was close to her ear, intimate through the sound of the rain.

She glanced up at him. His eyes glimmered so weary, burdened. "How many did we lose?"

"Twenty-one." The grief in his voice matched that in her soul. "That heifer's the only one that survived." He nodded toward the black calf, hungrily nursing from its mother. "I'm glad you saved her."

She couldn't stop herself from watching him—his profile, as he stared at the herd before them. His hand still lingered warm on her shoulder. Somewhere along the way he'd lost his hat, and rivulets of rain streamed down the strong planes of his face.

He turned to look at her then, those dark eyes conveying a message she couldn't quite decipher. But it made her breath catch. He was so close, only a couple feet away. His hand lifted from her shoulder and trailed up to her cheek, brushing back a soggy strand of hair that clung to her skin. "Have I told you how thankful I am for you?"

She couldn't breathe, couldn't speak past the lump in her throat.

"I need to get you in out of the rain." His voice rumbled

deeper than usual. His thumb stroked her cheek and she leaned into the touch. If he kissed her right now, there wasn't a chance she'd stop him.

Her eyes wandered down to his lips. She'd never realized how full they were. Never seen them this close. She forced her focus back up to his.

His gaze flickered, penetrating hers. Asking.

He must have found his answer, for he came closer. Closer. Those full lips found hers in gentle touch, a warm connection. Sweet honey.

As he pulled away, her eyes fluttered open, and she could only stare at him, the wonder of the kiss clouding her mind.

His hand slipped from her face, stroking down her arm and leaving a trail of fire everywhere it touched. He gave her hand a gentle squeeze. "Let's get home."

~

Monty could barely see Grace's outline as the group of weary cowpunchers rode home in the dark, yet he couldn't pull his focus from her. His fingers still ached with the softness of her cheek, cold and wet from the rain.

And the way she'd looked at him, it heated him to the core. He'd certainly not planned to kiss her. Not out in the rain, after the terror of the stampede and the devastation of so many promising calves.

But the moment he'd touched her, a connection pulsed through him. He'd barely made his decision, but she already had his heart, his head, and every part of him. Did she possibly feel even a little of the same? If that kiss were any sign, she felt something.

Soon, he had to get her alone. Just the two of them where they could really talk. Not out in the rain with the rest of the men close enough to interrupt. His mouth pinched. Had the boys seen that kiss? Between the darkness and the rain, it had felt like only the two of them existed in all of Texas.

But if they'd been observed, so much the better. He'd be staking his claim soon enough anyway.

~

On Saturday morning, Grace jogged down the stairs as the breakfast smells filled the air. She honed in on one particular aroma. Coffee.

The front door opened at the end of the hall, and Monty stepped inside. With the daylight streaming from behind him, she could see only the outline of his profile. Yet what a profile it was. He held more strength in those broad shoulders than the rest of the men put together.

As he closed the door and hung his hat on the wall peg, his face came into focus—along with that hint of a smile that pulled more on one side than the other.

It made her stomach flip every time. They'd not been alone for more than a minute since that kiss the night of the stampede, but the looks Monty sent her when the others weren't looking… Too bad she'd not taken him up on that walk last Sunday. But maybe he'd ask again. Soon.

"Morning." He stepped closer.

"Good morning." She should turn and walk toward the dining room, but something about his expression had her rooted in her tracks. What else could she say that wouldn't sound senseless? "Thanks again for the day off today."

A twinkle flickered in his eyes. "You're welcome. I'm headed into town this morning to drop off some things for Jacob. Would you like to ride along? I need to pick up supplies too, so I'll have the wagon. I can treat you to a real sit-down dinner at the Magnolia."

Her stomach flipped again, and the flutter moved up to her chest. A whole day? Just the two of them? Sounded like heaven.

But town? That familiar tightness found her shoulders and neck. Did she dare chance a trip to town where so many people would see her? So far she'd been able to avoid it. But there'd not been any sign of danger either. No evidence of Leonard. And how long had it been since she escaped California? Five months. Surely after five months, his anger had died down. His desire to steal what was hers.

Who was she kidding, his greed would last much longer on that score. But if she wore a dress to town, she would blend in with the other women. Nothing about her would be memorable if a stranger came to town asking questions.

She glanced up to meet Monty's gaze. "I'd love to."

~

Grace held the burgundy dress to her chest in the mirror and examined her reflection. The dark color was too formal for a Saturday outing. She tossed it on the bed and picked up her blue cotton. Even with the lace trimming, this was still more fitting for the day.

She stared into the mirror. What was she doing accepting this man's proposal, even for a simple outing together? She couldn't get involved with him. There was too much chance she'd have to run again. Leonard's connections spread too far. His greed ran way too deep to give up before he'd found her. Found the treasure.

But she couldn't let him have it, no matter what. To him, it meant only riches. But to her, it was her heritage. The very reason for her existence.

Turning, she padded to the bed and sank onto it, still clutching the dress to her chest. What was she going to do? Part of her wanted to go with Monty more than she wanted to breathe again. But was it wise?

No, definitely not wise. Could she get away with just today? She'd have to keep her distance from him. And keep her pistol tucked in her boot.

But she could do it. Just for today, she would allow herself to enjoy each minute as it came. But not get too close to the man by her side.

CHAPTER 13

Monty whistled the tune to "Sweet Betsy from Pike" as he cut a sideways glance at the woman on the wagon seat beside him. She sure was a pretty thing in that blue dress. Pretty enough to make him want to sit and stare. And he could probably get away with it too, because she'd not offered more than a single look and maybe a sentence or two since they'd left Double Rocking B property a half hour ago.

What was running through her mind? Grace had never been a magpie, but today her silence stretched between them like the width of the Rio Bravo. Had he made her angry? *Lord, I'm no good at this courting stuff. Is that why you've kept me from women all these years? Give me wisdom.*

He licked his parched lips to bring some moisture back into them. "Any place special you'd like to stop in town? I need to go by the mercantile and the saddlery. Other than that, the day's yours."

She spared him a glance, then turned back to the countryside as it eased past. "I don't know. The mercantile, sure. Maybe just a drive through the rest of the town to see what it's like. I've not been any closer than our round-up camp."

He studied her. "Not even before you joined on at the ranch?" How had she known where to find them if she hadn't come through town? The main road to the Double Rocking B fed straight through Seguin. Surely she hadn't been roaming the countryside and stumbled onto the ranch buildings.

She glanced at the horses and shrugged. She still hadn't met his gaze, but at least she didn't have her back to him now. "No, not through Seguin."

"So did you hear about our ranch in San Antonio?"

"I knew there were several ranches taking on help. The area looked nice, so I stopped in at the first place that seemed to be kept up decently well."

Not a direct answer, but he'd let it slide this time. He just needed to keep her talking. "How long was the trip from California?"

Her mouth pinched, hiding those full lips he could still taste. "About five months."

"Five months?" He didn't bite back the words before they slipped out. She could have walked from California in less time. "You must not have taken a direct route then."

She shrugged again, then glanced down at her hands. "Just saw the countryside."

Monty followed her gaze down. Her fingers were interlaced, clasped tightly enough to show white at the knuckles, but the thumbs played a back-and-forth game. First one on top, then the other. Was she nervous about something? Or bored?

Either way, the whole point of today was for her to have a pleasant time. He'd do well to find a better topic.

"Got a letter from Bo the other day."

She perked up and finally looked his way. "They made it home safely?"

He nodded. "Miranda's still feeling poorly, but he said the children asked about you."

"Asked about me?"

The corner of his mouth tugged into a grin. "Don't sound so surprised."

"Paul and Sandria were so sweet but…I didn't think they'd even remember my name."

He tightened the reins to slow the horses as the wagon picked up speed down a hill. As soon as he could spare his attention from the road, he turned to capture Grace's gaze. "You're a very memorable woman, Grace."

She blanched, part of the color slipping from her face. Uncomfortable with his words?

He pressed on anyway. "How could they not love you? It'd be hard for anyone not to."

There. He'd planted a seed. He held her gaze for another moment, the edge of his vision catching the steady rise and fall of her chest.

The road turned, and he had to move his focus back to steering the team. Let that give her something to think about.

~

The white limecrete wall around Seguin perched in the distance as Grace took in the view. She was almost sad to see the quiet ride with Monty end.

His words about her being memorable had spooked her, though. *Memorable* was the very last word she wanted to apply to herself. So memorable a passerby would recognize her from a description in a newspaper? She had no doubt Leonard had advertisements in every paper west of the Mississippi. Probably the eastern ones, too.

As they neared the opening in the whitewashed wall and the clean rows of buildings forming the pretty town, Grace reached under the bench seat for the stylish bonnet Anna had loaned her. "I suppose I should put this on so I don't embarrass you." And so she wouldn't be recognized as easily, although the brim of this hat barely shaded half her face.

A smile played at the corners of Monty's mouth. "You could have come in your vest and chaps and it wouldn't have bothered me."

Heat flamed up her neck before she had a chance to press it down. The way Monty's dark eyes soaked into her right now was not at all like a ranch foreman to a hired hand.

He parked the wagon in front of a building sporting "Theo Koch's Saddlery" in black painted letters across the front. "I just need to drop some saddles off, but you can come in if you like."

As Grace stepped through the open front door, the smell of leather wrapped around her. There was nothing quite like that wonderful, spicy aroma. She closed her eyes and inhaled, then opened them and moved to the closest saddle display. A rich mahogany color, with a star shape carved into the skirt on either side.

One by one, she examined every piece in the shop while Monty talked with a man behind the counter. Mr. Koch obviously had an eye for tooling leather, with many of his wares sporting decorative elements and designs.

After a few moments, Monty stepped up behind her, his presence soaking warmth through her even as her heart picked up speed. She held up a knife sheath. "Look at this, Monty. I haven't seen anything this elaborate since I left California. Some of our men from Mexico used to have ornate knife and gun holsters. Saddles, too. Sort of like that one." She pointed across the room to a vaquero saddle, complete with angled stirrup covers and all the trimmings.

He cleared his throat. "I have a saddle something like that. Haven't used it in years, though."

She spun on him. "You do?"

He looked a little sheepish. "Probably covered in dust and mold but…yeah."

After the saddlery, they walked over to Stewart's Mercantile. What a surprise to meet Anna's aunt and uncle there. She'd heard Anna had a small amount of family somewhere in the area, but hadn't expected to be introduced today.

When they stepped out of the shop, Grace touched her hat to make sure it was still in place and leaned close to Monty. "You didn't tell me we'd see people you knew here. I hope I looked presentable."

He touched his hand to the small of her back and leaned down. "You look beautiful and they loved you." The warmth of his breath touched her neck, sending gooseflesh across her shoulders.

She hazarded a glance at him, but the intense heat in his eyes took her breath. He was so close, less than a foot away. She forced her gaze down. Dangerous. Being so close to this man was way too dangerous.

"Are you hungry?" Monty's hand still rested on her back. The lightest touch, yet it warmed through her dress and chemise, all the way to her core.

She probably should have played the delicate female and said no, but after the long wagon ride to town, she *was* hungry. "A bit. Whenever you're ready."

He paused and scanned the street. Grace stopped too, but the abruptness of his halt made his hand slip from her back. She immediately missed the touch, but tried not to let it show on her face.

"We could eat at the Magnolia if you like. They have a nice dining room. Or…we could get a box lunch from the café and eat at the square. There's a pretty pleasure ground there with benches and a little pond."

She spun to face him. "Let's do, Monty. That sounds wonderful."

After purchasing sandwiches at the Bakery and Confectionary, they strolled toward the center of town. Several benches lined the expanse of grass around a small pool of water. Massive trees overhung several seats, pillars of wisdom that must have seen many decades of change in the town.

Monty pointed to one of the benches. "Does this look all right?"

Grace couldn't help but eye the massive trunk beside it. "What do you think about sitting there?" She turned to look at him. "Would you mind?"

One side of his mouth tipped up. "I'd prefer it."

It took real work to pull her gaze from that mouth. She could still feel the touch of his lips to hers. The nearness of him. Squaring her shoulders, she marched toward the base of the pecan tree.

It would have been easier if she'd worn trousers and not this infernal dress and petticoats, but she finally had the skirts straightened and positioned so she didn't show her boots. As if Monty hadn't seen them before...but still.

While they ate, Monty told her stories of when he and Jacob came to town as boys. She hadn't realized they'd been so close. Monty didn't come out and say it, but it sounded like he might have been the stabilizing force to Jacob's daredevil ideas. She couldn't help a grin at that. Everything about Monty was solid and reassuring. Like he could bear the weight of any challenge.

If only she could share her own struggles with him. But that was out of the question.

He asked about the area she'd grown up, and she did her best to describe the desert country, with its cactus and sagebrush and rocky bluffs. It took a lot more land to raise cattle there than it did in Texas.

"How far from town were you?" He leaned forward, cross-legged, and fingered a piece of grass while he watched her.

Grace rested against the tree trunk and sank into her memories. "It was a little over a half day's ride to the village of Santa Ana. We didn't go very often, maybe once or twice a year. Instead, Mama and Papa threw all kinds of rodeos and fiestas on the ranch for our men and the neighbors. We celebrated Carnaval, Día de Nuestra Senora de Guadalupe, Las Posadas, and lots of other holidays. The men took any excuse they could to celebrate." She allowed a soft chuckle. "I think they might have made up some of the festivals."

Monty's husky laugh joined hers, a low rumble in his chest that made her stomach flip. "Sounds like your growing up years were more Mexican than mine."

She met his gaze, and couldn't help sharing his smile. His eyes held such magnetism, especially when they sparkled like this. "Do you miss it?"

He raised his brows. "My upbringing?"

She wrinkled her nose. He was being obtuse on purpose. "Mexico."

Tilting his head, he studied her. "Can't say that I do. I was only twelve when I left, and things were so hard there. After my parents died, I left Bo with our cousins. Tío had so many mouths to feed already, I couldn't justify adding myself to the lot. Figured I was old enough to make my own way.

"So, I wandered around for a while, picking up odd jobs. Stumbled across the border to Texas without even realizing it. Jacob's pa found me in Seguin and offered me a job. I was pretty hungry by that point, and the Double Rocking B seemed a step better than heaven. I never once thought about leaving after that."

What a sad but incredibly touching story. "Have you thought about leaving now that you're grown?"

Monty met her gaze solidly. "No. I owe a lot to the O'Brien family. They'll always have my loyalty."

The passion in his voice was unmistakable, and something tightened in her chest. That loyalty—it was in her blood, too.

She didn't want to be always on the run. Always looking over her shoulder. She wanted a permanent home, like the ranch where she'd grown up. A home with a man she loved, working by his side. A man like Monty. The yearning washed through her with such force it stung her eyes.

She focused on Monty again and her breath caught at the expression in his gaze. Those windows to his soul were normally dark, but not this rich coal black, with heat that radiated through her. His focus wandered down to her mouth, springing up memories she couldn't fight. Her skin remembered the feel of him, the taste of him—wanted another.

He was closer now. Drawing even nearer. Her eyes drifted shut, more than ready for him.

As his lips touched hers, a warmth flooded through her. She drank him in. Kissing him back, sliding her fingers behind his neck, into his hair.

She'd been wrong. She didn't want a permanent life with a man like Monty.

She wanted *him*.

~

Monty bit back a groan as he pulled Grace closer. Nothing was close enough, though. She tasted like apples and cinnamon from the tart she'd eaten at lunch. He wanted more. Craved more.

Who needed this courting stuff anyway? Why couldn't they just go straight to the preacher? He loved Grace. She was his soul, he could feel it in every part of his being.

With the last ounce of strength left in him, he pulled away, resting his forehead on hers as their breaths mingled. "Grace."

She touched a finger to his lips, stilling his words. He nibbled the tip of it. There would be time enough for words. Time enough to make his intentions clear.

For now, he pulled her close, tight against his chest. He could feel the beat of her heart, almost as strong as the pounding of his own. After several moments, she sank into him, as if finally melting away the last of her resistance. He tightened his grip, his thumb stroking circles on her back.

Finally, at long last, he had the woman God intended for him. He could feel it in every fiber.

CHAPTER 14

Grace found herself once again admiring the tooled leather in Mr. Koch's saddlery while Monty settled up with the man at the counter. Through the single shop window, the freshly hitched team stood with tails swishing against summer flies. Soon they'd be starting the long ride back to the ranch. Almost two hours Monty said the trip took, although it hadn't seemed that long on the way in. Of course, the company had been pleasant.

She fought the urge to touch a hand to her lips. Monty's kiss had been…sweet molasses. The most perfect thing she'd ever experienced.

Her eyes drifted toward the window again. Wagons and men on horseback passed in a steady stream. Most looked like area farmers and ranchers. Today being Saturday, it must be a popular day to come to town.

In some of the wagons, women perched beside their menfolk, serviceable bonnets shading their faces so it was hard to gauge age or features. Other than Anna, it'd been so long since she'd known a woman's friendship. What would it be like to meet these ladies? To chat at church or visit during sickness. She swallowed. Those kinds of thoughts would get her in trouble.

She'd do much better to focus on the men passing by, always keeping a watch for anyone who bore resemblance to Leonard.

Like that man riding astride the stocky bay. From a distance, he looked remarkably like her step-brother. Same slight hunch to his shoulders, just barely tilted right from an old arm injury. He claimed he'd taken the bullet in defense of a lady, but she'd always thought it more likely he'd been called out for cheating at cards. Or maybe it had been a gunfight over a lady of the night. He'd never been shy about his activities there. Except, of course, when Papa or his mother had been around. He was smooth as freshly-strained milk when he wanted to be.

As the man rode closer, an eerie sense of familiarity crept over her. That hat. The way he held his reins in both hands, like he was afraid the horse would leap out from under him any minute. The brim of the brown bowler hat shaded his face so she couldn't make out any features from this distance.

She edged to the side of the window frame, yet didn't dare take her eyes off him. He seemed to be scanning the passers-by on the street, but not looking into store windows. And then he shifted, so the light hit his face, and cold bumps broke out across Grace's body.

It *was* him.

After five months and fourteen hundred miles, Leonard had found her.

"Are you ready?"

Grace jumped at least six inches at the words murmured close to her ear. She whirled, her hand reaching for the Colt at her hip, but finding only cotton fabric.

Monty studied her, head tilted and brows furrowing. "What's wrong?"

At least the startle had forced her heart into beating again.

Blood rushed through her with enough force to steal all her strength. She gripped Monty's arm when her knees started to buckle.

He grabbed her waist, pulling her back up and tucking her close to his side. "What's wrong, Grace?" The words were insistent, with an undertone of fear. "Are you sick?"

She forced air through her lungs, steeling her jaw against the lightness in her head. "I'm fine. Just...ready to go home."

He wrapped the other arm around her, snugging her tight against him as he turned toward the door. "I'll be back in a minute to get that saddle, Teddy."

The moment the afternoon sun hit her face, Grace ducked into Monty's side. What had she been thinking to walk out of the store in plain view of the street? She grabbed for the half-pint hat she'd borrowed from Anna. It barely covered part of her cheeks. Ripping the hat pin out, she pulled it forward so it shadowed her face.

"Grace, did you hit your head? Do you need a doctor?" Monty's voice held an edge of panic.

"No, Monty. I think my eyes are just tired from the sun." Not that she didn't work out in the sun every day. "Can we go home? Please?"

She'd slipped out of his hold when she turned to fix her hat, but he gripped her elbow again. "If you're sure."

By the time they drove through the white limecrete wall marking the outskirts of Seguin, numbness had taken over her body.

What was she going to do now? There wasn't really a choice.

She had to run.

And soon. If Leonard had tracked her to Seguin, he must have found a solid lead. One that could likely place her on the Double Rocking B.

But who could have seen her? Someone she'd passed in San

Antonio? She'd only spent an hour in that city before hightailing it back to her campsite in the woods.

Maybe it had been one of the men at round-up. In truth, that was the only other time she'd been off Double Rocking B property since she'd arrived. She couldn't imagine any of her fellow cowpunchers from the ranch would turn her in. No matter what pretty picture Leonard had spun about how he was trying to help recover his poor lost sister.

So she had to run. Tonight. And pray Leonard wasn't, even now, on the road ahead of them to the ranch.

But where would she go? North to Kansas? Abilene was said to be quite a city since the train started going through. Or east? She'd have to go pretty far to find a city large enough to hide in. Maybe all the way to the coast. But an eastern city? Where hundreds of people covered each block and she'd be forced to wear a dress every day.

There weren't cattle in a grand city. So what in the world would she do to support herself? She still had money saved from the small amount of cash Papa named for her in his will. Leonard and his mother had taken everything else. The ranch, the accounts—everything except the diamond. But that she'd never part with. Not ever, for any reason.

"You sure you can't tell me what's wrong?"

Grace jumped as the words broke through her thoughts. She turned and forced a smile for Monty. "I'm sorry, Monty. I'm all right. Really. Just tired."

He eyed her. "Is it something I said? Or...did?"

Oh, Monty. Could she really leave this man? A vice clamped around her heart and squeezed tight enough to send a burning sensation up her throat. "No. You've been wonderful. Today was wonderful. I'll always treasure it." The sting in her throat reached her eyes, and she turned away so he didn't see her weakness.

She'd need to find a backbone if she was going to leave. And she had to. Her family's legacy would be lost if she didn't. And maybe even the lives of those she'd come to love.

~

Something was wrong. And he'd be jiggered if he could figure out what.

Monty cut another glance at Grace as he turned the horses at the post signaling the entrance to the Double Rocking B. She'd drifted into another world, and nothing he said or did seemed to pull her back.

What had happened in that leather shop? One moment, she was looking at him like he'd gifted her a trick horse, and the next she was white as new snow and more wobbly than a newborn foal.

Some of the color had come back to her now, but she still looked...ill. There was no other way to describe it. He'd almost taken her to the doctor against her argument, but maybe Anna and Mama Sarita could help more than any male doctor.

He reined the horses to a stop in front of the ranch house, set the brake, then jumped down to help her. Grace was already clambering down the other side, though. In a few long strides he'd made it around the horses and gripped her elbow to assist.

She stopped and looked at him, the sadness in her eyes washing through him like a surging river. She pressed a hand over his where he held her arm. "I'm fine, Monty. But thank you. For everything."

The force of that look—those words—slammed into him, and he swayed a bit from the impact. So much that he could only watch as she slipped from his grasp and disappeared inside.

"You want I unhitch the horses, señor?"

"Si, Juan. Gracias." But Monty couldn't tear his eyes from the front door as it pulled shut.

And he couldn't shake the feeling something critical had just changed.

~

As soon as she stepped into her upstairs room, Grace dropped to her knees beside the bed. Reaching under, she grabbed the bedroll, then unfolded it across the bed.

Her fingers fumbled with the buttons down the front of her dress as she tried to make a quick change into her trousers and working clothes. She'd ride out after everyone bedded down for the night. Unless something happened before then to make it expedient—like Leonard showing up. She'd have to be ready for either scenario.

If she left in the middle of the night, would Georgina make too much noise and wake the men in the bunkhouse? Should she pull the mare out now and hide her in the woods somewhere? Or maybe she should pretend to go out for a short ride after dinner—and not come back.

No, Juan always took special care of her horse. He wouldn't bed down until the mare was safe and sound in the corral beside the barn. And if she was gone too late, he'd send out an alarm. The men would be on her heels before she made it to the next county. She'd have to take her chances leaving in the middle of the night.

She folded the dress and undergarments inside the bedroll, and tucked in the few supplies she had left. Matches. She'd need to gather enough food to sustain her until she was several towns away. Her violin case would ride strapped to the saddle under the bedroll. So that only left...

With unsteady hands, she pulled the velvet-wrapped bundle from where she'd tucked it with her undergarments in the drawer. Resting the treasure on the bed, she unwrapped layer after layer of protective quilting. She set the papers aside that told the story of the diamond, confirming its authenticity for over thirty years now. At last, the pocket that held the jewel secure. She slipped off the button hook and slid her fingers into the forest green pouch.

The stone inside felt solid—cold to the touch. She pulled it out and almost dropped the gem against the brilliance of the rays. Nearly blinding.

Sinking to her knees, she laid the pear-shaped jewel on the soft protection of its case.

There it was, the Ahmed Shah Diamond. Seventy-two carats of pure translucent crystal. One of the most coveted diamonds in the world.

Papa had spent his fortune to acquire it, out-bidding hundreds of other moguls at the sale in India. Outbidding even Mama's own father. And the outcome of that sale had changed their lives beyond what any of them would have imagined.

So many happy years the three of them had shared, even though Mama chafed under the remoteness of the California ranch. Especially compared to the English manor she'd been raised in. The diamond had been the catalyst for the wonderful life they'd lived.

Yet now that it was solely in her possession, the diamond had brought nothing but pain. If only Papa had never shared the secret with his second wife—if only he'd never married her to begin with.

Grace had tried to keep her distance from the woman once she took up residence at El Rancho de las Rosas, which hadn't been hard since she spent most of her time with the men and the cattle.

But she still couldn't quite reconcile Papa's death just six months after the wedding. So strange that he would be thrown from a horse, the same animal he rode long hours each day. And with Leonard the only witness to the tragedy.

She'd not had enough proof for the law. But proof wouldn't have brought Papa back to life. Nor Rusty. A tear slipped past the burn in her eyes. Everything dear to her had been lost. Except this diamond. She cupped her hands around it and stared into the sparkling facets.

A knock at the door nearly stopped her heart.

CHAPTER 15

"Who's there?" Grace fumbled to fasten the diamond inside its pouch, then wrap it back in the layers of quilted material.

"It's Anna. Just checking on you."

Grace's pulse thundered through her chest as she scrambled. "I'm all right. Just…a minute." She had to secure the diamond, then hide all her other packing. With clumsy hands she stuffed the re-wrapped diamond into her bedroll, folded it quickly, and pressed it under the bed with the violin case.

Lurching to her feet, she stumbled toward the door, caught herself, and paused for a deep breath. *Get yourself together.*

She was still in her stockinged feet, though her working clothes were all fastened properly. Padding to the door, she cracked it open.

Anna stood on the other side, head tilted and brow furrowed. "Grace?"

She tried to summon a smile. "Yes. I'm fine, Anna. Just worn out from the trip to town. Thought I'd rest some."

Anna didn't look convinced. "Monty said he thought you were ill."

Monty. Why did he have to care so much? A lump lodged in her throat. "Just a headache. A nap will have me good as new."

Anna's gaze roamed over her, then settled back on her face. "Can I get you something? Dinner will be ready soon. How about if I bring up a tray?"

The mass in Grace's throat crept upward to sting the backs of her eyes. Anna was becoming such a good friend. How hard it would be to leave these people. Would they think her ungrateful? Think she'd lied? She hadn't really lied, had she? Just not told all of her story. Not let them know she'd be leaving in the dead of night when danger drew near.

But it was for their good as much as hers. Leonard would be ruthless in his search. If Anna or Monty or any person tried to stop him, he'd not hesitate to dispose of them. Just like Papa.

She swallowed hard. "No need for a tray. I'll rest for a while, then come down and roust up a snack. You don't need to worry about me, Anna. I promise." And that would give her an excuse to gather food supplies.

"If you're sure." Anna's mouth pinched.

"I'm sure. Thanks for checking."

As Anna walked away, Grace closed the door and sank against it, her knees almost buckling. That was much closer than she should have cut it. Did Anna suspect something? She surely thought it was strange Grace didn't invite her past the threshold. But hopefully she'd chalk it up to exhaustion.

Turning, Grace moved back to her belongings and quickly finished securing the bundle.

There. Everything was ready now, save the food. She scanned the room, her eyes landing on the bed. Maybe she should take a nap since she wouldn't be sleeping tonight.

But as Grace curled on her side in the cozy bed, her mind began to torment her. Not with thoughts of Leonard—that would have at least put some starch in her backbone.

The face that came alive behind her closed eyes belonged to Monty. Her mind replayed that kiss, her traitorous body reliving every part of it. Why had she let down her barriers enough to allow it? But she didn't really regret it. That kiss was one she'd take with her and savor forever. The memory that would likely spoil her to any future connections. No man could ever come close to Monty.

A pang sliced through her chest, spilling out in a tear that slipped down her cheek. How could she have come to love him so much in such a short time? Would he hate her after she left? Would he think she'd only used him, then moved on?

Oh, God, no. Please don't let him believe that. Leaving Monty would be bad enough, but making him think badly of her…

Grace jerked up to a sitting position. She had to tell him. Otherwise she'd spend the rest of her life regretting her choice. Even if she couldn't say where she was going or why, she'd tell Monty what he'd meant to her.

Slipping into the chair at the desk, she pulled a piece of paper from a drawer and picked up the quill. As she stared at the blank parchment, thoughts swirled in her mind. So much to say, but would it be too much?

~

Monty eyed Grace's empty chair at breakfast the next morning as he took his second bite of boiled oats. The gruel burned down his throat, settling in a lump in his gut.

Anna had said Grace was merely tired last night, although he'd have bet a month's wages it was more than that. Surely she'd checked on Grace this morning. Would Anna have come to find him if Grace still felt poorly? She was his hired hand after all, he needed to know if one of his people was sick.

Pushing back from the table, he strode toward the kitchen

where Anna's voice murmured amongst Emmaline's chattering. He stepped through the doorway, and both voices halted.

"What is it, Monty? Do you need more toast or oats?" Anna's innocent gaze stared up at him from the small kitchen table where she snuggled baby Martin.

He stepped closer and lowered his voice so the men didn't hear in the room behind him. "Is Grace ill?"

Her brow knit in innocent confusion. "I don't think so. Is she? I haven't seen her yet this morning."

His jaw clamped against the fear rising in his gut. "She's not at breakfast. Haven't you checked on her?"

She rose to her feet, bouncing the babe as he let out a squawk. "I'll go see now."

He didn't offer to hold the youngster, wasn't sure he'd be decent company at the moment. But he did follow Anna out to the hallway and watched her ascend the stairway.

At the top, she gave him a wry glance, then disappeared down the hall. He strained to hear sounds from above. A soft knock, the murmur of Anna's voice, the creak of the door.

His heart pounded a steady gallop in his chest. Something had to be wrong with Grace for her to skip breakfast. Meals were important, especially the morning grub, and every cowpoke with a week's experience knew that. He'd be sending someone for the doctor this morning whether Grace wanted him to or not.

Anna's face reappeared at the top of the stairs—white as the paint on the wall. "She's not here, Monty."

He tilted his head, the words not sinking in the way they should. Surely she was up there. If not, where would she be? Maybe in the barn?

Whirling, he strode toward the front door. "I'll see if she's in the barn."

"Monty." The quiver in Anna's voice caught him up short.

He eased around to look at her. "What?" That gallop in his chest froze to a dead crawl as ice took over his veins.

"Her clothes are gone from the drawers." She held up a folded paper. "This was propped on the bed."

As if he'd slipped into a dream, his body moved forward but his vision grew hazy—distant, like he was watching from somewhere overhead.

When he took the paper, it felt stiff in his hand. Turning it over, he had to blink several times before his eyes registered the single word written on one side.

Monty.

He raised his gaze to Anna, the meaning of it all still not quite sinking through the fog in his brain. "This is for me? What did she write that she couldn't say to me herself?"

Anna propped the baby higher on her shoulder and nodded toward the note. "Open it."

The words were enough to penetrate his mist like a blistering sun. He fumbled with the wax seal holding the paper shut, then opened the folds and scanned the paper. A neat feminine script jumped out at him, covering three-quarters of the page.

Monty,

I'm very sorry, but I have to go. My reason has nothing to do with you or the ranch, but pertains to what forced me to leave California. I'm afraid that's all I can say about it, but I couldn't go without telling you how much you've come to mean to me.

You, Monty, are one of the best men I've ever known. Your character, your loyalty, and your strength surpass all others, and have broken the barriers I'd built around my heart. I shouldn't be writing this, I know, but as much as my heart breaks at the thought of leaving you, it would shatter completely knowing you thought ill of me.

I hope that is not the case. Please know I wouldn't leave unless it were absolutely necessary. I hope you can find the grace to forgive me.

Yours,

Grace

He stared at the words, emotions roiling in his gut. Then he read them again. She was gone? She'd really left the ranch? And what was she saying about her heart? If his eyes could be believed, she'd all but said she loved him.

Elation sluiced through him. But it died away as the slow burn of anger took over, boiling up as his focus landed on one of the final sentences. *I wouldn't leave unless it were absolutely necessary.*

The tiny hairs on the back of his neck raised on end. He'd known it since that first day Grace arrived. She'd been in trouble, and he'd lulled himself into a false security once he got to know her.

Who was threatening her? It had to be a threat for her to get spooked so suddenly, but how had she gotten wind of renewed danger? He thought back to their day in town. She'd seemed a little distant when they first left in the morning, but warmed up quick enough. And at lunch, she'd been more than open. That kiss... His body responded now to just the thought of it.

But after they left the saddlery...no, it was while they were in the shop she'd turned white as an albino. When she'd been looking out the window.

"Monty?"

He blinked at Anna as she shook his arm. "What?"

"What does the letter say? Is she all right?"

He glanced back to the paper in his hand. "I'm not sure. Where's Jacob?" He pushed past her. They had to make a plan. He'd go after Grace, sure as shootin', but they needed to be smart about this.

~

"So you don't have *any* idea who might be after her?"

Monty paced the small open floor in Jacob's office. Jacob sounded frustrated, but it didn't come to half a hair compared to the passion boiling in his own chest. "I don't know. She talked about her pa's ranch. Her ma died several years back, then her pa about six months ago, if I recall right. She mentioned a foreman who was like part of the family, but said he passed a while back, too. She talked about the rest of the cowpunchers like they were all kinfolk. Never had an ill word to say about any of them."

"So she didn't say why she left California?" Jacob watched him from his stance by the window.

Monty closed his eyes and inhaled a long breath, forcing his mind to remember every conversation. There had been more than he'd realized through the months. Most of them just snippets as they rode out to the herd or back, but each one mattered.

"All she said was there was nothing holding her there." His brow wrinkled. "She said she left California five months ago. When I asked why it took so long to get to Texas, she just said she'd been seeing the countryside. I thought that was strange, but I didn't push her." He scrubbed a hand through his hair. "Shoulda followed my gut."

A knock sounded on the door, and they both turned as Juan poked his head in. "Sí, the señorita's horse is gone and all her things from the barn. Is hard to tell, but I think I see fresh tracks going north and to the east."

"Gracias." Monty spun back to Jacob even before Juan shut the door. "I'm going after her Jacob. I'll be back when I find her." Hopefully, that wouldn't be long. No telling what time she'd left, but travel would have been slow at night.

Jacob stepped forward and rested a hand on Monty's shoulder. The strength of his friend's grip was unmistakable, and he met Monty's gaze head-on. "You want company?"

Monty took a moment to think through his answer. It would be good to have back-up in case they ran into trouble, but as he eyed Jacob, the reality of the possible danger glared back at him. He had no idea what he'd be walking into. He couldn't put Jacob through that. Couldn't endanger his best friend's family.

"No. I'll bring her back here, then we'll decide the next move."

Jacob pierced him with those intense blue eyes. "Be careful then. We'll be praying for you both."

Monty nodded, accepting the charge along with the prayers. Something told him he was going to need them.

CHAPTER 16

She was completely vulnerable.

Monty gazed through an opening in the branches as Grace slept in a little clearing in the woods. She'd traveled farther that day than he'd expected, and must have collapsed here around dusk thinking she was safe in such a remote place. If she thought that rifle beside her would be enough protection, she was sadly mistaken. He could easily snatch it before she pried open an eyelid. At least she'd had the good sense not to build a fire.

He couldn't help but watch her sleep, though. In the soft evening light, her face almost shone with its beauty. Those strong cheekbones and even stronger chin. With her eyes closed, her long lashes lay peacefully against her cheeks. So delicate. His fingers itched to touch her again. To stroke the softness of her skin. Kiss her eyelids. Her lips.

For a few more moments, he allowed himself the luxury of just watching. Someday, she would be his. As soon as they made it through this bit of trouble, he'd not waste any more time.

Tensing his muscles, Monty scanned the surroundings one more time. There'd been no sign of another set of tracks as he followed her, but someone watching might have traveled off to the side. He'd have to stay on his toes.

Stepping into the clearing, he padded on the balls of his feet to make as little noise as possible against the rotting leaf floor of the woods. He crept closer to Grace, then crouched beside her and pulled the rifle from her reach. No sense in her shooting him if she startled awake.

Her breathing kept a steady rhythm, ruffling a tendril of escaped hair draped across her chin. So peaceful. So vulnerable. Something in his chest squeezed tight. He reached out to brush her cheek with the backs of his fingers.

Like a snake strike, her hand closed around his wrist, clamping tight enough to catch him off guard. Her eyes popped open—even wider when recognition flashed in them. She released his hand and clambered up to a sitting position, scooting back a bit in the process.

"Monty. What are you doing here?" Her whisper echoed through the dark woods.

"Coming after you." He matched her volume, his voice as low a rumble as he could make it.

She twisted both directions to scan the trees, then focused on him again. "Why? What's happened?"

"Nothing yet. But you're gonna tell me what's going on, then we're going back to the ranch to work it out together."

Even with the scant bit of moonlight that made it through the trees, he could see her eyes widen and her head shake vigorously. "I can't, Monty. I can't do that to you." She scooted backwards again, and tucked her legs underneath her like she was going to jump up and run.

"Grace." He touched her arm, and she stilled. "You have to tell me what's going on."

She was quiet for long moments, and she'd backed into the shadows so he couldn't make out her expression. Her arm muscles were tense under his hand.

"Please, Grace. I need you to trust me." He needed that more than his next meal.

"It's my step-brother." The words came out so quiet, they were almost smothered in the night. "He's come after something of mine that he wants."

Monty shifted from his crouch into a seated position, settling in for the full story. Because they weren't leaving here until he knew all of it. "If it's yours, why does he think you'll give it to him?"

"He knows I won't, but he'll try to take it by force. It's very… valuable. And he's the kind of man who doesn't let anything get between him and what he really wants. I think he's killed before but I can't prove it." Her voice quivered with passion as she spoke. "I couldn't stay and risk something happening to you or the others on the ranch so… It's better if I move on."

He forced himself to stay calm. "Mind if I ask what's so valuable he'd take a life over it?"

"I can't tell you, Monty. It's better if you don't know."

Inhaling a deep breath, he examined the picture forming in his mind. "Something happened to make you think he's found you?"

A motion in the darkness must've been the nod of her head. "I saw him through the window at the saddlery. I don't know how he traced me to Seguin. I've been wandering around for months to cover my trail. But he has plenty of money and lots of connections in the west."

"Grace, I need to know what exactly he's after. I need to understand why he'd be willing to kill over a possession that doesn't even belong to him."

"It was my inheritance from my father. Papa left the ranch and most everything else to his new wife and Leonard, but what he left me is worth far more. That's why Leonard wants it. He's a greedy, manipulative…" She let the sentence die off, but the bitterness in her tone said more than enough.

"You said you think he's killed before. Do you mean...your father?"

"Yes." The whisper barely carried to him.

"Oh, Grace."

And then she was there. In his arms, a sob wracking her tiny body. He closed her in, stroking her back and inhaling her scent, the depth of her pain splintering his own heart.

Emotions warred within him—the ache of sadness mixing with a growing fury toward the man who would strip this woman of everything she loved. Her father, her home, her very safety. Leaving her with no alternative but to live like a criminal, hiding and skulking from one remote setting to another.

Well, no more.

Together, they would stand up to the man. And she wasn't leaving the Double Rocking B again until she very well pleased. Never—if he had anything to do with it.

At last, the sobs turned to sniffles and she tried to pull back.

He didn't let her go far, though. Just enough so the moonlight touched her face. He thumbed her cheek. "Listen to me, Grace Harper—"

"Hampstead."

He blinked. "Come again?"

"My family name is Hampstead. Since I'm telling you everything."

Of course it was. The faintest glimmer of a smile touched one side of her mouth. He fought the urge to swoop in and kiss it.

"All right. Grace Hampstead. We're going back to the ranch, and together, we'll take care of that slab-sided blighter. We have plenty of men there handy with a rifle, and they won't let him within fifty yards of you." For emphasis, he leaned forward and planted a kiss on those lips.

They parted just a bit in surprise, but he resisted the urge to deepen the kiss. Here in this remote forest in the dark... His willpower was strong, but even he had his limits. Besides, now might not be quite the time, what with the bit of worry about her life being in danger.

Pulling back, he studied her face again, wishing he could see more than shadows in her eyes. "I love you, Grace. I'm not going to let anything happen to you."

"Oh, Monty."

Her hand came up to his cheek, and he suddenly wished he'd taken the time to shave that morning. Turning into her touch, he kissed the soft inside of her palm.

"Do we have to go back? Maybe we could just stay here." The smile came through her words in a blissful sigh.

Take the deuce but she was making this hard for him. With a groan, he pushed her hand away. "Don't tempt me."

Glancing around the space, he struggled to focus on what had to be done. "I'll saddle your horse while you pack up."

"There's nothing to pack..." Her words faded into a yawn, stilling Monty before he started to rise.

"You need to sleep a bit before we go anywhere. I'll sit and watch for a few hours while you catch a nap."

"I'll be all right." But her argument was swallowed in another yawn.

He leaned forward and pressed a kiss to her forehead. "Sweet dreams. I'll be right here."

~

Leonard studied the ranch buildings through his spy glass, the same thing he'd done for two days now. The grounds had fallen silent in the afternoon sunlight, just like yesterday.

The old Mexican disappeared into the bunkhouse—for his siesta, no doubt. The nap had lasted over two hours the day before. If he'd counted the men correctly, the rest were out in the fields while only women occupied the house.

No sign of Grace, but this was definitely the ranch the driver had described. If she was hiding inside, he'd find her. Otherwise, he'd get her whereabouts from these yokels.

The fellow who'd hung around the place yesterday had ridden out with the cow hands that morning. That left only the boy in the barn and the two women in the house. Perfect.

He twisted the spy glass shut, then tucked it into his saddle pack and mounted his horse. The gelding surged forward before Leonard settled in the saddle, and he snatched the reins to still the animal. He'd made this horse into a decent riding steed on the trip from California, but after standing around these two days, it seemed the beast had lost his manners.

Moving into the lane, Leonard schooled his profile into a relaxed pose. As he rode into the ranch yard and dismounted, the boy jogged from the barn.

"Can I take your horse, sir?"

Leonard scanned the house and buildings as if he'd never seen them before, then focused a smile on the lad. "I'll lead him into the barn for you. He can be a bit finicky about who handles him."

"Yes'r."

He kept his posture relaxed, but scanned the area one more time. Still no movement around any of the buildings. Perfect. The solid form of his Colt pressed into his side, ready for the next step in the plan.

The interior of the barn was so dim, it took a moment for his eyes to adjust.

"We'll stick him in here." The boy stopped at one of the first stalls. "You want him unsaddled?"

Leonard stepped close behind him. With a practiced motion, he pulled his revolver from his waistband and slammed it into the back of the boy's head.

The lad crumbled like the backbone had been pulled out of him. Good.

After settling the gelding in the stall, Leonard made short work of tying the boy to a wagon wheel in the back corner. He gagged him, too. Just in case.

Now onto the house.

The yard was still quiet as he crossed it, mounted the porch steps, and rapped on the door. A woman in a green dress answered—the younger one he'd seen coming and going the most while he'd watched the house.

"Hello." She eyed him warily.

He removed his hat. "Hello, ma'am. Is the man of the house around? I've some business I'm hoping he can help me with."

Her brown eyes narrowed. "Can you come back this evening? He'll be better able to talk then."

He raised a brow. In this god-forsaken country? What did she expect him to do, ride the two hours back to town and wait in the café? "Perhaps you could help me instead." He motioned into the house. "Would you mind if we sit to discuss the matter?"

She glanced over her shoulder, licked her lips, and turned back to him. "I...suppose."

As he followed her into the hallway and through a side door to a sitting room, he eyed her tense movements. Was she nervous by nature? Or had Grace alerted these people to possible trouble?

He'd be on his toes, but after studying the workings of this place for two days, he was pretty sure he had the upper hand. *That* was probably what made her so jumpy. She knew she was unprotected.

She motioned him toward a settee. "Please be seated. I'll have coffee brought in."

"No need. If you'll join me, I'll explain my business."

She perched on the edge of the seat across from him, her hands clasped tightly in her lap. "Yes?"

"Well, ma'am. I've been on the road for several weeks now, looking for my sister. She was kidnapped from our ranch in California and I have reason to believe she was taken as far as central Texas." He pulled the sketch from his pocket—the drawing he'd used on the wanted poster. "Here's a likeness of her. Perhaps she looks familiar?" He studied the woman as she took the paper.

"You say she was kidnapped?" Something about her tone, the patronizing arch of her brows, told him without a doubt she knew Grace. And she'd likely been warned he'd be coming. No telling what slandering hogwash Grace'd sold these people about him.

"Yes, ma'am. Have you seen her?"

Since she'd already been prejudiced against him, there was no need for him to go into his prepared speech. Either she would tell what she knew or he would find it for himself.

She looked up from the sketch and looked him square in the eyes. "I have no idea of this woman's whereabouts."

He forced a crestfallen look. "Has she been here at all?"

"You'd best look elsewhere."

Enough talking in circles. He rose to his feet, and she did the same. Turning his body to hide his movement, he slipped his hand into his waistband and withdrew the Colt.

The look in her eyes as he turned the business end toward her was priceless. Just like a startled deer. "Madam. You will tell me where Grace Hampstead is, or I'll not hesitate to enforce the alternative."

Eyes as wide as plates, she shook her head decisively. But the fear was there. She'd break soon enough.

"Is she here now?"

Another violent shake of the head.

"Where did she stay when she was here before?"

The woman's jaw clamped shut.

With the reflexes he'd honed through years at the poker table, he landed a left hook squarely on the side of her stubborn jaw.

She let out a cry and jerked back, pressing a hand to the spot where he'd connected.

He re-leveled the gun on her. "I asked a question, madam."

Her glare was cold, but he'd seen a great deal worse.

"Where's the old lady then? Perhaps she'll be more likely to tell."

"Grace stayed upstairs, but she's long gone. You won't find anything." That glare again. Did she think it would make a difference?

"Thank you." He nodded and stepped back to allow her to pass, keeping the Colt's barrel pointed at her. "If you'd be so kind as to proceed toward the kitchen."

If he didn't miss his guess, that's where they'd find the old lady, too. Either there or napping upstairs. Either way, he'd get them both out of the way and find what he'd come for.

CHAPTER 17

As Leonard pushed the woman through the kitchen doorway, the grey-haired female was just where he'd expected—standing over the sink slicing something. She put up a little fuss, but he soon had them both tied and secured to the legs of the cold stove. He gagged the older woman first, then waved the pistol toward the younger. "Which room did you say Grace occupied? It'll save me from searching them all."

"Turn right at the top of the stairs. Second door on the left." The words were almost indiscernible through her gritted teeth.

He tied the rag in her mouth, then stepped back to eye his work. Everything in place so far. Now it was time to find what he'd come for.

The room the woman described was neat as a pin. Nothing in the drawers, in the bedding, not anywhere. No sign Grace had been there at all. After slashing through the mattress to make sure she hadn't concealed a hint there, he scanned the room one more time. His search had been thorough—everything he did was thorough—but still turned up nothing.

Forcing his rage into a tight ball, he scrutinized every corner of the other two rooms down that wing. Both looked barren when he began, but quite the mess when he finished. And still…nothing.

His patience was starting to wane, and the rage harder to contain. After all this time, he'd found where the chit had been hiding out. And now there was no trace of her? Absolutely not to be borne.

A burn boiled in his gut. If they were hiding her somewhere, he'd find the imp. Time was running out before the men would show up again. He had to move faster. Charging through the remainder of the house, he jerked open doors, turned over beds, kicked aside cabinets—anywhere she could be hiding.

Still nothing.

How dare she run from him, after all he'd offered the ungrateful brat? Instead of the ranch that had been her birthplace, she'd chosen a sentimental gemstone she never intended to sell. What a stupid waste of millions of dollars.

He *wouldn't* waste that money. Not when he had men already on the hook. A buyer waiting in India. Not when this was the only source of income large enough to satisfy his creditors and set him up for life. He would *not* lose this chance.

In one of the final rooms downstairs, he did find one interesting thing. A baby.

For a moment, he watched the sleeping boy. It had to belong to the younger woman tied in the kitchen. How could he use this to his advantage? It would certainly draw information from her.

A quick search of that chamber revealed nothing else. Before he left the room, he gave the crib a solid kick. The infant jerked, then let out a wail.

Leonard spun on his heel and stomped from the room, a tiny smidgeon of satisfaction easing the burn in his gut. His purpose would be accomplished much faster if she were forced to hear her brat cry.

Storming back into the kitchen, he extracted his hunting

knife from its sheath at his waist. He snarled at the woman, piercing her with his anger. Not a hard look to conjure at this point in his search. "Where is she?" He jerked the cloth out of her mouth.

The babe's cry drifted from the other room, and the woman sat up straighter, anxiety washing over her features. "I don't know. She left in the night with no word where she was going."

He stepped closer, brandishing the knife not far from the woman's face. "When?" He knew it wasn't last night, because he'd been watching.

"A few days ago."

Straightening, he eyed the blade in his hand. Tapped the point of it so a tiny bead of blood sprang to his finger.

The baby's cries wailed louder. The tendons in the woman's throat constricted as she swallowed. The little urchin was actually helping. Maybe he'd go easy on the sniveler.

Meeting the woman's gaze with a cold glare, he tapped the flat of the knife blade. "Madam, if you value the life of that squalling brat in the crib, then you will tell me where Grace went and exactly when she left. Every. Detail." He enunciated those final words so they left no doubt in her mind.

She licked her lips, but didn't speak. Didn't whimper or anything. *Now* she was going to make a show of bravado? When her child's life was in danger? Perhaps she thought he was bluffing. Time to prove otherwise.

Spinning on his heel, he'd only strode two steps before her cry stopped him.

"No! I'll tell you everything."

Finally. He turned back and raised his brows.

"She left two nights ago. Didn't tell us anything was wrong, just left. We discovered her missing the next morning. One of our men found her tracks on our property going northeast. I don't know where she went after she left here. She never said anything about leaving or where she would go. I thought she was here to stay. I promise."

The words spilled out in such a rush, she couldn't have formulated a lie that quickly. He eyed her a moment longer. "You have anything else to share?"

Anger flashed across her face, but then her lower lip found its way between her teeth. Good move if she'd planned to fire an insult.

Now for his next steps. Grace obviously wasn't here, but at least he had a direction and a time frame. And that time frame burned in his throat. One night sooner. If he'd been here one night sooner, she'd have stumbled right into his grasp.

Grabbing a lantern from the table, he slammed it against the counter near the old lady, shattering the glass casing and bringing out a little scream from the woman. Kerosene sprayed across much of the wood. He didn't see any other lanterns in sight so that would have to do the job.

These women had accomplished his purpose, although they'd certainly not made it easy on him. But he knew better than to leave behind a trail of accusers. It was time to put an end to them. He grabbed a match from the shelf over the stove and swiped it against the metal range.

Impatience sluiced through him. He was here to get the diamond, not fuss with women and children. With a flick of his wrist, he tossed the flame onto the kerosene-soaked wood, then spun toward the door.

Time to take action.

As he strode past the chamber where the babe's wails filled the air, a niggle of remorse touched his chest. He wasn't crazy about killing the innocent. But the cow hands would see the smoke soon and come running. They'd find the child in plenty of time before the fire reached it.

Leonard shook off the concern as he slipped out the front door.

~

Monty slanted another glance at Grace as they turned from the main road onto the track leading to the ranch buildings of the Double Rocking B. She'd been quiet on the trip back, especially these last two hours. But if her drooping eyes could be believed, it was more exhaustion than reticence to come back.

As he watched, her eyes narrowed even more, and her back straightened. "Monty, does it look like something's different about the house? Look at the corner where the kitchen is. That's a lot of smoke for a cook stove."

He jerked his attention to the sprawling log home. It was debatable whether the smoke was excessive, but a tightness clenched his gut anyway. Had Leonard already found them? Surely Jacob had the place protected.

Still, he plunged his heels into Poncho's sides and cantered toward the buildings. Grace was close on his tail as he rode around to the back of the house, right up to the kitchen door. A smoky haze filled the air now, carrying a strong scent of kerosene. In two leaps he was up the stairs and jerked the door wide. It took a second for his eyes to adjust to the mixture of flame and dim, smoky air.

"Monty!"

The cry jerked his attention, and he made out a figure struggling in the far corner. He lunged that direction and squatted in front of Anna and Mama Sarita.

"Untie us." Anna twisted to expose her hands strapped to the base of the stove. Mama Sarita did the same, although she also wore a cloth gag through her mouth.

He was barely aware of movement from Grace near the fire as he pulled out his knife and sliced through the ropes holding the women to the stove. How did the stove get out here in the corner, though? It was usually beside the counter, much closer to where the flames licked almost as tall as Grace.

As soon as he freed Anna, she scrambled away. Mama Sarita did the same, although a bit slower, as though she'd been sitting in the cramped position too long. How long?

He couldn't worry about that now. They had to fight the blaze before it grew unmanageable.

As he joined Grace, she dumped a bucket of milk over the flames, smothering a small section. "I'm out of water," she yelled over the crackle of the fire.

"Use these." Anna pushed through from behind, shoving a blanket at each of them.

Adrenaline surged through Monty's veins as they beat the fire into submission. With each heave of the blanket, his mind spun. This had to be Leonard's work. A kitchen fire he could understand, but not the women tied to the stove. And where was Jacob? The children?

Panic seized him as he whirled to find Anna. "Where are the children?"

She motioned behind them, and Monty followed her gaze to Mama Sarita, standing in the doorway with baby Martin in her arms.

The wave of relief almost melted the strength in his knees. But that only accounted for one. Spinning back to where Anna rubbed her blanket over the ashes on the wall, he asked, "Emmaline?"

"She spent the night at the Wallace Ranch."

He closed his eyes against the letdown of adrenaline. *Thank you, Lord.*

Grace beat out the last of the flame, and turned to Anna, touching her arm. "Go to your baby, we'll take care of this."

Monty watched the look that passed between the two of them, and it only intensified the burn in his chest. They'd both been in so much danger—were *still* in so much danger. The man had to be caught.

Anna moved to where Martin still whimpered in the older woman's arms, and Monty stepped back to survey the scene. "Where's Jacob? And Juan? The rest of the men?"

"Jacob went out with the cowpunchers." Her brow furrowed. "I'm not sure about Juan. He might be hurt." Her voice rose as the realization settled over her.

"He's probably napping. I'll go check on him." Mama Sarita patted Anna's shoulder in a calming gesture, then disappeared toward the front hall.

As Grace finished beating the hot ashes from the charred skeleton of the dry sink, she straightened and turned to meet his gaze. The intensity there was almost palpable. A flare of the same anger and determination that raged through him.

He'd not been here to help, and the result had nearly been disaster. But there was no way he'd rest until this man was made to pay.

~

The knot in Grace's stomach tightened as she swept her gaze over the smoky mess in the O'Brien's kitchen. All because of her.

Leonard had to be stopped. She was tired of running. Tired of dodging his moves just in time. But this time she'd failed. Innocent people she cared about had almost lost their lives. The panic that thought brought on would consume her if she let it. But now was definitely not the time to lose her wits. She had to keep a knife-tip focus.

Turning to Monty, she met his gaze for a moment. His thoughts were clear. He planned to stop the blackguard who did this.

But how?

Her gaze swept to Anna, bouncing and crooning to her baby in the doorway. The look of exhausted relief on her face spoke to the trauma she'd been through.

Grace hated to regurgitate those memories, but she just needed a little information. "Anna, how long ago did Leonard leave? Do you know which way he went?"

Anna looked up from the babe, tucking her cheek against his head, although she never stopped the light bounce. "I'm not sure how long ago. Felt like forever, but we couldn't have been tied long or the fire would have spread farther. As soon as he lit the blaze, he left in a hurry."

"Do you know which way he went?"

Anna's gaze dropped. "I…I told him you'd gone northeast." She looked up again, her gaze pleading. "I tried not to. I wasn't going to give you away, Grace, honest. But he had us tied and had a knife out and said he was going to hurt Martin." She curled deeper into the warmth of the baby. "He'd already ransacked the house, so I thought he really might do it."

Grace was by Anna's side in two strides. "Anna, it's all right. I'm so, so sorry you went through all that. Both of you." She stroked the soft down on the back of Martin's head. "It wouldn't matter what you told him, Leonard would have located me eventually. Just like he found me here." She glanced over her shoulder at Monty. "It's time we take care of him for good."

She turned back to Anna with the warmest smile she could summon. "Go care for the baby. We'll be right out here."

No sooner had Anna disappeared into her chamber, than the front door flew open and three figures hobbled in. Grace strode forward, Monty close on her heels. It took a second to make out the profiles with the light shining from behind, but Chester's chattering voice helped with the recognition.

"I was just pointin' out the stall an'—wham! The next thing I knew I was out."

Mama Sarita had an arm draped around the boy, and a sinking feeling pressed in Grace's abdomen. He'd been hurt?

She reached Chester and settled a hand on his free shoulder. "What happened?" A glimpse at Juan showed deep worry lines, with a hint of bewilderment.

It took several minutes and a couple of ginger cookies from the pantry to get the full story from the boy. Through the recounting, the anger in Grace's chest grew, mixing with fear. How much these people had suffered on her account. It couldn't happen again.

"Juan, ride out and tell Jacob what's happened. Have him bring at least half the men in." Monty had taken on his role as leader again, and the firm decisiveness in his voice took away a small measure of the fear churning in her chest. It was hard not to feel safe in this man's presence.

The wrangler left straightaway, and Chester seemed to have worn down some of his excitement, as a yawn seeped out of him.

Grace touched the boy's shoulder. "I think you should go lie down, but not in the bunkhouse by yourself. In case you take sick from the blow. Why don't you rest on the settee in the parlor?"

"Yes'm." The boy must be feeling fairly miserable to give in so easily.

As he dragged himself toward the front room, Grace turned to survey the damage in the kitchen again. "I guess I should clean until the others get back."

Monty stepped up behind her, strong arms wrapping around her waist as his chin settled on top of her head. The warmth of his touch, the solid strength at her back—it was her undoing.

She sank into him, a burn welling behind her eyes as a sob escaped.

"Sshh…" He turned her face into his shoulder, and she clutched his shirt, gulping in deep breaths. "It's all right, honey.

It's gonna be all right." Monty's fingers stroked her back without loosening his grip around her.

She soaked him in. The aroma of pine and horse and man, all rolled into the essence of Monty. And with his touch and nearness, she gradually regained control.

When she finally stepped back, she wiped at her eyes and sniffed. "I'm sorry." She couldn't force herself to meet his gaze, though.

Monty touched her chin, raising it as he ducked down to her eye level. "We'll get him, Grace. With God's help, he'll be locked up by this time tomorrow. And then all this will be behind us." His thumb reached up to brush another errant tear, threatening her control all over again.

With a deep breath, she turned away. She straightened her shoulders, then set to work cleaning.

CHAPTER 18

"We have to leave now, Monty. Every minute he's getting farther away."

Monty's gaze tracked Jacob's pacing across the office. "You don't think I know that? But if we don't have the sheriff with us, it's our word against his if something goes wrong out there. This man hasn't had a crime stick to him yet, and I'm not taking any chances. He'll pay for what he's done here."

Jacob released a frustrated grunt. "But what if we lose his trail? It'll be dark in a few hours." He spun on Monty. "Worse yet, what if Leonard realizes her trail circles back to the ranch? I don't want him back here, Monty. Not under any condition. Not even if we have a whole regiment of cavalry guarding the place. I *will not* put my family through that again."

And that was the ace card. Monty clamped his jaw tight as the image Jacob painted came clear in his mind. "All right. We'll ride out now. I can try to draw a map of the trail Grace took for the sheriff to follow." Assuming Leonard could track well enough to follow the path she'd taken.

But he and Jacob would be following the man's trail. Even if it varied from the map, all the sheriff would have to do is follow their fresh tracks.

He leaned forward. "I'm thinking we take two men—Nathan and Jesse. We'll leave at least four others posted here at the house, and the rest out with the cattle. There's no telling what he'll do if he thinks he's about to be caught, and I wouldn't put a stampede past him."

"Blast the cattle. He can have 'em all as long as he stays away from my family."

Monty raised a brow. Not that he could blame his friend for a bit of passion when he'd almost lost his wife and son to this villain. "The cattle are pastured near the house. The men on the herd can double as lookouts."

Jacob released a long sigh. "Let's go then."

Monty turned to the office door, his mind running through everything they'd need to take. As he pulled it open, he stopped cold as his gaze found the figure leaning against the opposite wall.

Grace.

Jacob bumped into the back of him, and Monty stepped to the side for Jacob and his nervous energy to escape. But he never took his gaze from Grace.

She pushed off the wall, squaring her shoulders. Even in the shadows of the hallway, her chin had that stubborn jut he'd seen so many times when she faced off with a cantankerous longhorn. "Do we leave now?"

She planned to go with them? Over his dead body. "*We're* leaving now." He emphasized the *we*. As in—not her. "Jacob and I will ride with Nathan and Jesse. I'll draw a map for the sheriff to catch up with us."

If it were possible, she drew herself up even straighter. "I need to go with you, Monty. None of you have seen the man. I know him. I can help."

"Grace, no." What was it with everyone wanting to argue

about this mission? But he was not backing down on this one. "You're not going and that's the end."

If she'd been a porcupine, she'd have thrown every one of her needles at him with that glare. He wasn't changing his mind though.

"I need to be there. If you don't let me ride with you, I'll leave on my own. Your choice."

A bolt of icy dread shot through him. She'd do it, too. She'd already proven that.

Monty turned away and scrubbed a hand through his hair. "You're killing me, Grace. You're really going to be the end of me."

She stepped closer, and a hand touched his upper arm, tentative. "I'll be all right, Monty. And careful. I just…need to be there. It's my fault all this happened to begin with, I need to take care of it."

He looked back and studied her. "How about if you bring the sheriff when he gets here? You can show him the route you took to begin with. I'm assuming Leonard's following both our tracks." At least that way, if they rode into a trap, she'd be in the second wave. And safe.

~

Monty scanned the tree line that surrounded three sides of the clearing they rode through. They'd settled into pairs. He and Jacob in front, Nathan and Jesse just feet behind. Each with a rifle in one hand, aimed at the woods around them. It'd been slow going for the first few hours, Leonard's trail had veered a few times from the path he and Grace took. And it'd taken time to sort his tracks from those of the local ranchers and their cow hands.

With their tracks so fresh, Grace and the sheriff shouldn't have the same trouble. If Santiago had been able to find the lawman right away when he reached town, Grace and the sheriff would likely catch up to them within an hour or so. His gaze followed the set of shod tracks in front of them, but he kept his ears strained for the whistle Grace had promised to send out before they approached.

They were just entering another copse of trees when that whistle sounded. Even if their trail had been obvious, this was sooner than he'd expected. Had they just raced to catch up without any concern for safety? The muscles in his shoulders tightened as he strained to make out the forms behind them through the trees.

Grace's outline sent such a flurry through his chest, the knot in his stomach balled tighter. He offered a tense smile as she brought her mare to a stop beside him.

"Miss Harper filled me in on your excitement." The sheriff's loud whisper broke through his thoughts, and Monty turned to face him. "Any idea how much farther ahead he is?" The man's long mustache twitched with each word.

Monty glanced up at the dusky sky. "Close I hope. We need to catch up to him before dark or it's gonna be a lot harder to follow the trail. Saw fresh droppings in that last field, so I'm prayin' he's not far."

The sheriff nodded. "Let's get to it, then."

Monty allowed the man to take his place at the front beside Jacob, while he dropped back to ride with Grace in the middle of the group. As they wound deeper into the woods, he kept as constant an eye on her as he did scanning the area around them.

She had a white-knuckled grip on the reins with her left hand and the pistol in her right. Did it shake, or was that the motion of her horse? The tense profile of her jaw and poker-straight back spoke quite a bit about the state of her nerves.

He eased his horse closer. "It's going to be all right, Grace. God has this already planned out." The words were as much for him as for her, but a quiet reassurance filled him as he spoke. If only he could take her hand and infuse the same confidence into her.

She glanced at him, her gaze catching on his as vulnerability flashed across her face. The dusky light in the woods masked her eyes, but he could imagine the intensity there. "How can you know that?"

It was the first time she'd asked a question about faith, and she'd not picked an easy one. Monty inhaled a breath. "For one, He says in the Bible He has control of what happens to us. But He's proven it to me so many times. I know God has this already worked out for our good. The hard part is the trusting."

She brought her gaze forward, and he couldn't read her profile. Was she hearing any of it? Or were her nerves so tied up, she couldn't focus? He knew she'd been raised in a Christian home, but there was a sight of difference between memorizing the catechism and trusting God as you're walking into the fire. Did she have the connection with the Father that would make that kind of faith possible? *Be with her, Lord.*

The faintest sound drifted from ahead.

"Stop," Monty whispered, and reined in. There it was again. An animal tromping through the leaves of the forest floor.

"Spread out in a U shape and see if we can surround him." Monty issued the command in a low tone as he reined his gelding to the side. Too late, he realized he probably should have waited for the sheriff to give orders.

But the men—and Grace—obeyed. Even as his senses heightened for the attack, he realized the plan carried Grace the opposite direction from him. He wouldn't be close by to protect her. *No.* Should he call her back to him? Have her switch places with Nathan? She'd be angry as a mama cow at weaning, and probably wouldn't do it. *Lord, protect her.*

With effort, he pulled his focus back to the work ahead, weaving his horse through the woods at a jog and fighting off branches. He kept Jacob just within his sights ahead.

If only they could get close to the man without him hearing. That wasn't likely, though. Not with a pack of six horses charging through the woods. Their only possible hope could be surprise and the fact that Leonard would have to weave around the same trees they did. But if he had a head start…

Within minutes, a figure appeared through the woods ahead and to the right. A bay horse.

Riderless.

"He's on foot!" Jacob's cry pierced the air as Monty glimpsed a figure darting away from the animal.

He pressed his gelding faster. Ducking and bobbing as branches struck.

A shot rang through the air. The blast came from somewhere up ahead, but it was impossible to tell who had fired it.

Monty reined in at Jacob's horse, and leapt to the ground. His friend had already dismounted and crouched behind a tree. Monty found a spot behind a neighboring oak—a good stout tree at least three feet thick.

"Did he fire the shot?" His whisper carried the distance to Jacob.

"Yeah. Felt the breeze from it, so I figured this was a good place to face off."

"Where is he?"

"Behind that cypress tree about thirty feet over."

So close? It was a miracle Monty hadn't been shot riding up. He forced in a deep breath. What now? Peeking around the trunk, he spotted the cypress Jacob must have meant. A huge sprawling thing with an impression in one side where Leonard must be hiding. The way he was tucked into the tree's indentation, he was shielded on three sides. They'd have trouble getting into a position to shoot him out without getting shot themselves. If the man had food and bullets to last him, he could hole up there for days.

Maybe they could talk him out. It'd be worth a try. Monty gathered his nerve and a breath.

"Leonard?" His call resonated through the woods, as everything settled into silence except the hard breathing of the horses.

"Who's there?"

The voice came smooth, self-assured. Like a seasoned gambler confident in the cards he held. Monty ground his teeth.

"I'm sheriff in Seguin, and you're under arrest." The sheriff's voice rang out before Monty could answer. Good. Let the lawman do things nice and officially.

"What charges could you possibly have against me? I've done nothing illegal."

Monty's gut clenched as anger sluiced through him. A snarl drifted from Jacob, but Monty sent him a glare. They had to keep their heads through this or someone would get hurt.

"Arson. Attempted murder. Destruction of property. Should I keep going?"

"I'm afraid, sir, you have the wrong man." That voice was so suave it made Monty's stomach roil. What a slimy, two-faced snake.

"You are Leonard Fulton, are you not?" The sheriff—always so steady and matter-of-fact.

Silence for a moment. "I am. Although, I've not done those things you accuse me of."

Liar. Monty dragged in deep breaths to still his pulsing temper.

"What's your business in these parts?"

Monty shifted from one foot to the other. Did the sheriff plan to talk the man to sleep? Because this conversation didn't seem to be going anywhere helpful.

"I'm looking for my sister. After our father died, she lost some of her faculties and ran away. I'm trying to bring her home to safety."

A strangled sound—half snarl, half war cry—echoed from what had to be the direction of Grace. "You mean *my* father. He was nothing more than a victim to you. You murdered him to take the diamond, but when that didn't work, you've hunted me down like a prize bearskin. Only now you've caught yourself in your own trap." The venom in her voice was unmistakable.

"Grace?" For the first time, the weasel's voice wavered from its suave security.

Monty peered around the tree. If the sheriff could keep the man's attention occupied, maybe he could get to a better position. There was a scattering of larger trees in the area that should be enough to cover him.

He turned to catch Jacob's eye and motioned his path. "Cover me," he whispered just loud enough to carry.

"You have thirty seconds to come out with your hands up." The sheriff spoke again. "Else I'll give these men the high sign to come in and get you."

Their chances would be much better if Monty could get a better angle. Inhaling a deep breath, he lunged from behind his oak and sprinted to a pecan about ten feet away. Adrenaline coursed through him as he reached his goal and peered around the edge to the cypress hiding their target. He could just see the edge of black cloth tucked in the nook of the tree. Possibly enough exposed to nick the man, but not enough to do real damage. But a few well-placed shots would certainly spook him.

Raising his Winchester, Monty sighted down the rifle's barrel and waited for his cue.

"This is your last chance, Fulton." The sheriff again.

The fabric tucked behind the Cypress shifted. Was the man planning to run? Monty would drop him at the first movement. There was no way Leonard Fulton would roam free to torment another person. Especially not Grace.

A shot ripped through the air, tensing every one of Monty's

muscles. The cloth disappeared—the man must have pressed himself closer to the tree.

Monty aimed into the wood just to the side of where the shirt had been and pulled back on the trigger.

Bark around the spot exploded. A sharp cry of surprise blended with the echo of the bullet. Leaves rustled at the base of the tree, dropping Monty's focus down to the two boots peeking out.

Perfect. He called out to the man, "Throw out your guns first, Fulton, then step out with your hands raised. Else I'll pick your toes off one by one."

A brief moment of silence followed, and Monty cocked his rifle.

"I'm coming out." Leonard's unsteady voice was followed by a pistol tossed through the air. It settled about five feet away from his tree.

"Throw the rest farther," Monty called.

A rifle landed a few feet past the handgun.

"Your knives and any other weapons."

A hunting knife came next. "That's all."

Monty didn't move, but kept the rifle aimed. "You sure? Cause if I find you're hiding something, I'll use it on you myself."

"Wait." The slimy invertebrate was whining now, but he threw out another smaller handgun. "That's everything."

"Come out with your hands straight up." Monty fingered his trigger, but forced himself to relax his white-knuckled grip some.

A lean man stepped from behind the cypress. His mussed brown hair and wiry mustache looked like he'd started the day with pomade, although the hair spiked out in tufts now. His tie and waistcoat peeked out from under a fitted black dress coat. What a dandy.

"Boys, I'm comin' out to apprehend the man," the sheriff

called. "Don't shoot me." Smart man with five cocked guns pointed at the scene.

Leonard kept his hands away from his sides as he sent Monty an evil glare. Then he glanced toward the oncoming sheriff.

Monty relaxed his grip on the rifle and rotated one shoulder to loosen a cramped muscle. The sheriff approached Leonard, metal cuffs already in hand. Out of the corner of Monty's eye, another figure appeared beyond the sheriff.

Grace.

He raised his head to tell her to get back, but in a flash, Leonard spun and aimed a tiny handgun at Monty.

An explosion ripped through the air.

Monty ducked as a cold sensation blew past his face. He jerked his rifle back up and sighted down the barrel.

"It's mine!" Leonard's scream echoed as he whirled and aimed the pistol at Grace.

Fear coursed through Monty as he squeezed his trigger, but his aim was off.

More shots exploded. Screams rent the air.

Grace.

He cocked again and raised the rifle to fire, but the sheriff lunged toward the criminal and took him down in a heap. More yells echoed as the lawman flipped Leonard like a sack of flour, onto his stomach with hands twisted behind him.

"My arm!" Leonard cried.

With the ruffian on the ground, Monty jerked his gaze away and searched the spot where Grace had been.

Nothing.

His heart pounded in his ears and he sprinted toward the place she'd been standing. "Grace!"

When he reached the spot, he whirled, eyes searching every direction. "Grace!"

"Monty."

The voice clutched his chest, and he spun to face it.

Grace stepped away from a tree, like an angel shimmering from the heavens.

He was striding toward her before he realized it. Running.

She lowered her gun and threw herself into his arms. He clutched her tight, dragging in deep breaths and soaking in the blessed scent of relief.

It was long moments before he could pull himself away, even to look into her face. But when he did, the exhausted relief—the edge of fear—clenched his heart in a powerful fist.

He pulled her close again, squeezing his eyes tight. She was safe. She *was* safe. He had to repeat the words over and over in his mind until the claw in his chest loosened its grip.

Grace let out a shuddering breath, then eased herself away. "The others… We need to help."

The cold that rushed in to replace her warmth felt like another blast to his chest. He tucked her into his side, and together they turned to face the group clustered around the form on the ground.

The sheriff kneeled atop Leonard, both knees pressed into the perpetrator's back as he worked the key into the locking bar of the manacles. Nathan and Jesse hovered over the pair, rifles trained on the man still writhing under the lawman's grip.

The blighter wouldn't have another chance to do more damage. He'd left marks deep enough already.

Monty glanced over at Jacob, watching the scene from a distance with his own rifle still aimed and ready. The tight expression in every one of his features said it'd take some time for him to wind down from the ordeal.

As he and Grace stepped closer, the sheriff shifted his weight off the man's back. "There. That should hold nice and tight. Any other weapons we need to know about, Fulton?"

"No, but my arm," Leonard moaned, his eyes shut as the side

of his face pressed into the leaves and dirt of the forest floor. "I'm shot."

A rip in the man's coat showed crimson soaking the cloth underneath. The man was still breathing just fine, though. He'd be all right for a while.

As the sheriff searched for any other hidden weapons, Monty looked up at his men. "Jesse, keep your gun pointed at him until the sheriff tells you different. Nathan, fetch the man's horse. Unless we'd rather have him walking back, which is fine with me."

"Horse is lame." Leonard's words were barely decipherable with his face pressed into the ground.

Nathan stepped back. "I'll go check him."

If Leonard's horse wasn't able to carry him, how exactly could they get the man to town? Unless some of them stayed out here in the woods overnight and hoped the animal was better in the morning. That would depend on the severity of the injury, though. He could easily believe Leonard had pushed the horse too hard for the conditions. The horse could have stepped in a snake hole in the dim light of the woods and broken a leg.

"I guess we can put him on my horse. I could ride with you."

He turned at Grace's soft words. She'd be willing to let the man use her horse after all he'd done to her? Not that he was complaining about the thought of having her tucked behind him all the way home. That might be the best possible way to travel, now that he thought about it.

He scanned her eyes for any hint of fear. With the darkness falling deep in the woods, shadows threatened her eyes. What he could see was only bravery, though. "Maybe. Let's see how bad the animal's hurt."

Night had overtaken the forest completely by the time they were all mounted and heading home. Fulton's horse seemed to have only a stone bruise, but it was enough to slow their ride to a crawl as the animal limped behind.

Fulton was strapped onto Grace's mare, with his hands in irons and a gag firmly fixed over his mouth. That'd been the only option to get the man to quit blabbering. The sheriff rode on one side, with a firm grip on Fulton's reins. Jacob rode guard on the opposite side, his rifle across his knees and a hand within easy reach of the trigger. Nathan and Jesse rode up front, scouting the trail and blocking in Fulton in case he tried to do something really dull-witted.

Monty tightened his grip on Grace's hands as they encircled his waist. Her head rested on his shoulder, body pressed against his back. The steady reassurance of having her there—safe—was just now starting to ease the tension in his muscles.

Could this whole awful ordeal really be over? He breathed out a long, cleansing breath.

Thank you, Father.

CHAPTER 19

Grace stepped onto the porch in the pre-dawn darkness and wrapped her arms tighter around herself. It'd been a couple hours since she'd ridden back to the ranch yard with Monty and Mr. O'Brien. Nathan and Jesse had agreed to accompany the sheriff to town to make sure Leonard was locked up tight.

She was supposed to be sleeping now, collapsed into exhausted slumber like the rest of the household. But she couldn't bring herself to face the bed yet. Seeing Leonard had called up too many emotions she'd worked hard to squelch. That grimy feeling she always had when he looked her way. The day he'd come riding back to the ranch with Papa's lifeless body.

Tears burned her throat and eyes, but she braced both hands on the rail and forced the moisture back. It'd been almost a relief to flee the ranch after living a month alone with her step-mother. Without Papa to temper the woman's greed and sharp tongue, she'd been impossible.

Coming here to the Double Rocking B had been like finding home again. And Monty. She'd never felt so alive as when he was near. Yet the shadow had still hovered over everything that was good. Fear that Leonard would find her—a shadow that sucked the edge of joy.

Could it really be over? What had Monty said yesterday as they rode through the woods? *God has this under control. The hard part is in the trusting.*

She stared up into the dark, cloudless sky. God was there, she didn't doubt it. But could she trust that he had Leonard's fate under control? *Her* fate?

The rail took her weight as her knees started to give way. If she trusted God with the diamond—her birthright—did that mean she had to trust him with every other part of her life, too? Could she?

He's proven Himself so many times. Her mind drifted back through the events of the last year. The twelve months that had seemed like the disintegration of her life. Yet the picture formed differently this time. Had God been directing the events to bring her here to this ranch? This little slice of heaven? And Monty?

A movement rustled on the path, and she tensed, ducking behind a porch support. Not that the four inch post would hide much of her.

"Grace?" Monty's voice, gentle as it drifted through the night.

Her muscles relaxed, and she clutched the column to keep from sinking to her knees. Where had all her strength gone? "Monty."

His boots clicked softly as he mounted the wooden steps, his outline slowly forming from the blackness. "Can't sleep?" His deep tenor washed over her like a warm blanket in the coolness.

"Not yet. You either?" She could see parts of his face now, although much remained steeped in shadow. It couldn't hide his gentle strength, though.

"Thought I'd take one more look around before I bed down." He came to rest beside her. Less than a foot away—close enough for her body to crave his touch. She didn't close the gap, though. "What's on your mind?"

She forced her thoughts to focus on what had occupied her so thoroughly just minutes before. "I was thinking about what you said on the trail, about God having a plan through all of this."

How could she put into words the turmoil in her heart? The desire to trust, yet the fear of it. "I think I can see it. It's just… harder to trust when I can't see everything that's to come."

"It wouldn't be trust if you could see it."

She turned to look at him, warmth spreading through her chest. He had such an easy way of stating the truth. A clear perspective. "I want to trust, Monty. I'm ready. I think."

He slipped an arm around her waist and pulled her close so her head rested on his shoulder. "That's the best news I've heard all day."

Her mouth pulled as she fought the grin. "The day's still young."

They stayed like that for a while, her head resting against him, their heartbeats melding into one. She'd never felt so…at peace.

The blush of dawn touched the eastern horizon, filtering a dusky magic over the ranch yard. She finally pulled back and scanned his face. "So where do I go from here?"

He kept one hand at her waist, but the other came up, fingers brushing her cheek. "No matter what, God has you tucked in his hand. And I have a strong feeling that he brought you here for a reason. For me, Grace." His thumb stroked her jaw, and the breath stopped filling her lungs. What was he saying? "Would you do me the great honor of becoming my wife?"

The words took several seconds to register, like a fog had infiltrated her mind. His wife? Sweet heaven. But did he know what he was asking? This was Monty, man above men. Could he really want to tie himself to her?

His face seemed earnest, but she had to ask anyway. "Are you sure, Monty? You would want to marry a woman who wears trousers and works like a man? I'm not sure I could ever be a normal housewife. Not the woman you deserve."

A corner of his mouth lifted. "You're the woman I've dreamed about for months now. Since the first day we met. I didn't even realize the kind of woman I wanted until God brought you to me. Whether you wear trousers or not is your choice." His thumb touched the corner of her mouth, sending a skitter all the way through her. "I like the idea of you working alongside me, but only if you want to."

The warmth in her chest spread through every part of her, expanding her heart so it was impossible to hold back a smile. "I'd like to, Monty. Although it might be harder after children start to come."

His face slackened for just a moment, as though the fog had crept into his brain too. Then his dark eyes glistened in the dawning light. "I like the idea of children."

Without another word, he lowered his mouth to hers, finishing the thought with a promise as old as time.

~

Monty dragged open his scratchy eyes as a yawn took over his entire face. Daylight filtered through the muddle in his mind, and he sat up straight. He'd overslept.

But then the events of the last couple days crashed over him, pressing him back down to the pillow. What a whirlwind it'd been. Ending with…

The memory of Grace's words and that kiss took over, pressing it all aside. She'd said yes. God be praised.

They'd not talked about the details yet. As soon as the others started stirring, he'd sent her straight to bed.

How soon could they set a date? Maybe he could talk her into having the ceremony this Sunday. He'd go get the preacher today if she'd agree, but she probably wanted a church wedding. Or did she? He should know better by now than to try to think for Grace Harper. Or Hampstead, rather.

No matter. Soon enough she'd be Grace Dominguez. His wife.

Pushing up from the bed, Monty scanned the bunkhouse, reality sinking in like a bucket of cold water. They couldn't be married yet. He had no house to bring her to. That cottage he'd dreamed about in the next clearing over would have to become a reality now. And soon.

But that would take weeks. Months.

His head dropped into his hands and he pressed the heels of his palms into his eye sockets. "Lord, you're killing me."

The old bunkhouse on the other side of the barn flickered through his mind, but that was no place to bring a bride. Just one open room with a cook stove at one end. Stark as a newborn bunny. Even with the holes in the roof patched, there wasn't a chance he'd bring Grace into that shack—no matter if it moved the wedding up by a couple months.

Pulling on his boots, Monty stood and splashed water on his face from the tin washbowl. Donato had told him not to go out with the others to the cattle today, but it was time to see what needed doing at the main house.

There was the usual bustle of activity through the front rooms. Anna rocked the baby in the parlor while Jacob played some kind of marble game with Emmaline. The child jumped up when Monty stopped in the doorway, and she flew into his legs with a squeal.

Jacob rose a bit more slowly, old man that he was becoming, and strode toward them with a tired grin. "Thought you were gonna sleep 'til dinner."

Monty glanced at the parlor window, but couldn't get a read on the time of day. "You already eat lunch?"

"A couple hours ago. But you're not the only one. Grace hasn't stirred yet either."

Monty's chest did a little flip at her name, but he did his best not to let it show on his face. He glanced past Jacob to examine Anna. "You feelin' all right today?"

Anna's head lolled against the back of the rocker and she gave him a soft smile, the sleeping baby cuddled against her shoulder. "Thankful."

A lump filled Monty's throat and he had to swallow hard to push it down. "All of us."

"You should see my new kitchen. The boys are doing quite a job on it."

Monty turned to Jacob, raising his brows. He knew Santiago fixed the stove last night, but figured it'd take a bit before they could repair the damage to the wall and work counter.

A little hand gripped Monty's and pulled. "Come see, Uncle Monty."

Jacob nodded that direction, so Monty allowed Emmaline to pull him down the hall. His gaze wandered up the stairs as they passed, but all seemed quiet up there. Grace must be exhausted for sure if she could sleep through all this clamor.

Male voices drifted from the kitchen as they neared the doorway. Emmaline tugged harder, hopping and skipping as she entered the room. "See, Uncle Monty? I got to help paint the wall."

As Monty took in the scene, Santiago and Carlos paused in their work to watch him. Each man held the end of a shelf, and Santiago also gripped a hammer in his right hand and a nail between his teeth. The wall behind the shelf, which had been covered in crumbling ash yesterday, now shone a bright white-wash. The stove fit neatly in its original position, as if it had never been dislodged by two terrified women. How had they accomplished so much just today?

"The new counter's finished outside, but the paint's still drying on the legs." Santiago had removed the nail from his mouth to speak. "Mama Sarita said it would be nice to have more shelves, so that's what we're building now." The one they held had curved endbells fitted on either side, shaped almost like a scroll.

Monty raised a brow at his cousin. He'd known the man dabbled in carpentry back in Mexico, but hadn't seen him produce anything in years. "Nice job."

"Do you want a gingersnap, Uncle Monty? Mama let us all have them after lunch, but we saved some for you and Miss Grace." Emmaline ran to the pantry and pulled a cookie from under a cloth.

"Thanks, little bit." He tousled her hair and slipped half the cookie in his mouth. The moment the spicy flavor hit his tongue, his stomach took the opportunity to remind him he hadn't eaten since the sandwiches Mama Sarita set out for them last night.

Jacob's chuckle drifted from behind him. "There's probably something in there that'll stick to your ribs, too."

Monty eyed the pantry shelves, then glanced at his friend. "You have a minute to talk while I eat?"

Ten minutes later, Monty sat at the massive pecan-wood table in the dining room, thick slices of ham and tomatoes piled on sourdough bread before him.

Jacob perched to his left in Donato's usual chair, arms extended across the table. "So what's on your mind?" Just like Jacob to get right to the point.

Monty fit his mouth around the oversize sandwich and savored the bite while his friend waited. A little patience never hurt anyone. And how exactly should he share the news? Just come out and say he'd be marrying Grace, or work up to the topic? Straightforward was usually best with Jacob O'Brien.

He swallowed the last of his bite and glanced at his friend. "I asked Grace to marry me this morning."

Jacob took in the news with raised brows arched over wide blue eyes. Then with a hoot, he slapped the table. "Well it's about time, old man. I'm assuming she said yes?"

Monty only responded with his own raised brow, although truth be told, he'd been a little worried about Grace's answer himself. He hadn't really meant to ask that particular question before she'd had a chance to recover from the ordeal with her step-brother. But standing there in the dawning light, it had seemed like the right time. Especially after she'd shared about her faith and wondering what her next steps should be.

A slap on the shoulder brought Monty back to the present—and Jacob's wide grin. "So what's your plan for a house? You wanna build here by us? Or the next clearing over?"

Even though he'd expected as much from Jacob, a bit of tension left his muscles at the automatic way his friend assumed he'd be sticking around. Putting down even deeper roots in this ranch that was already part of his soul.

"I was thinking the next clearing over if you don't mind. I'd like to take Grace to look at it when she feels better."

"Definitely get the woman's opinion." Jacob gave him a droll look. "If you've learned that trick, you'll live a long and happy life. Wherever you guys decide, just let me know and I'll deed you the acreage around it."

A ray of warmth seeped into Monty's chest. Deed the land? He'd hoped only for the chance to erect his own house on the O'Brien property. Like a sharecropper. Instead Jacob was offering him permanence—a treasure to be tended and passed to future generations.

A lump formed in his throat, and he raised his gaze to meet Jacob's squarely. "That'd be nice."

CHAPTER 20

Grace matched her stride to Monty's as they stepped through the tall grass at the edge of the clearing. The pinks, oranges, and blues of the sunset cast a magical tint over the land, draping it in warmth and comfort. The perfect spot for their home.

Monty slipped his hand into hers, intertwining their fingers and pulling her close.

"It's perfect, Monty. Absolutely perfect."

"You like it? I was thinking maybe the house could go there, facing the trail. Maybe a shed off to the side for wood and such. Or a barn if you'd rather."

She pulled to a stop in the middle of the area where the house would sit, then motioned toward the eastern corner. "It'd be nice to put the kitchen here where we can watch the sun rise over coffee in the mornings." Glancing his way, she caught his gaze. A warm, fluttery feeling glided up her chest.

"A couple of the boys have offered to help build in the evenings. I'll go to town for a load of wood on Saturday, but we can start felling trees before then. I'm thinking we can probably have it dried in with a bit of furniture in a couple months." He turned her toward him, slipping his hands around her waist. "I hate to wait so long, but we'll be working as hard as we can to finish sooner."

She searched his face. He was concerned about something, but what? "Will it be all right for us to stay at the main house until then?"

A line formed across his forehead. "You mean stay the way things are?" Confusion muddied his gaze. "I'd rather not, but don't see much other choice."

Something about his words didn't quite ring clear in her mind. "The way things are? You mean not have the wedding?" Surely he wasn't saying he didn't want to marry her.

He cocked his head and studied her for a moment, then his brows shot up. "You mean we get married now and stay at the main house until this one's ready?"

What had he been thinking? That they wouldn't marry until after the house was built? Heat flared into her face. Land sakes, he must think her a hussy. Or at the very least, desperate.

He threw his head back and let loose a chuckle, and Grace tried to pull away. He didn't relax his grip at her waist, but instead pulled her closer as he lowered his forehead to hers. "I like your idea better. I kinda wanted to have a home ready to bring my bride to. But if it doesn't bother you, I won't complain."

The warmth of his nearness had its usual effect on her heart, pushing it into a steady gallop. "I'm just going to let you handle the details from here on out."

Another deep chuckle resonated from his chest. "We're in this together."

~

Monty scanned the room, taking in the cleaned-up bunch of cowpunchers packed into the front parlor of the Double Rocking B's ranch house.

Soon, this wouldn't be the only home on the ranch, just the *big house*. And having Grace tucked away in their little cottage would be all right with him.

Bo's son, Paul, squirmed in his mother's grip, and Bo scooped up the lad.

Not that Monty could blame the boy. He fought his own urge to squirm. Maybe pull one end of his string tie and loosen the chokehold. What was taking the women so long?

A throat cleared behind him and Monty glanced over at Jacob's raised brow. A grin tugged at his friend's mouth, but the look only sent an extra shot of nerves into Monty's gut. It was finally happening.

His wedding.

Even though the men were packed like cattle in a loading pen, it seemed right to hold the ceremony here in the parlor. The place he'd first met Grace.

It'd been her idea. Even though she'd come to church and town with him these last couple weeks, this was where she felt most at home.

A rustle near the door caught his attention, as Mama Sarita slipped into the room. A sliver of anticipation wriggled through his chest, and Monty clasped his hands behind his back to keep them from fidgeting.

Anna appeared next and gave him a sly smile before she stepped across the room to stand beside the place reserved for Grace. But where was his bride?

After staring through the doorway to the empty hall for several moments, the knot in his stomach tightened and he shot a look at Anna. She, too, stared toward the opening. But she didn't look worried. That had to mean everything was all right. Didn't it?

And then, like a ray of pale blue sunshine, Grace stepped into the room. The entire place lit as if she brought the daylight with her. She wore the blue gown he loved, but something about it seemed different. A bit fancier maybe. With her hair piled up in curls and lace, it accentuated the delicate strength of her face. And her long slender neck.

And those eyes.

Lord have mercy, those eyes spoke to him like nothing else. And just now they were fastened on him with a look that warmed him clear to his toes. Her mouth held a soft smile as she drew close.

She stopped just feet away, and he reached for her hand. They should turn and face the minister, but he couldn't quite pull his gaze from her. Not yet.

When she squeezed his hand, he squeezed back and did his best to hold in the giddy grin that took hold in his chest.

Together, they turned to face the preacher, but Monty didn't let go of her hand. Against all odds, God had brought them to this place, and he planned to enjoy every minute of it.

As they spoke their vows, Grace's words were sure and steady. Much more so than the gallop in his chest. But one sentence the reverend spoke caught and held in his mind.

"Therefore, what God hath joined together, let no man put asunder."

As Monty pulled his bride close for their first kiss as husband and wife, he paused to take in the love reflecting in those crystal blue eyes. It so perfectly matched what overflowed in his own chest.

~

It felt like forever before all the backslapping and well-wishing was over. Anna had wanted to throw a big fiesta to celebrate the marriage, but Grace talked her into only a few of the traditional Mexican wedding foods.

Which suited Monty just fine. They'd have plenty of years to celebrate with the others, but today belonged to the two of them.

Like the faithful friend he was, Juan had their horses saddled and waiting by the time Monty was able to sneak Grace away from the festivities.

They mounted, and cantered from the ranch yard by way of the back corral behind the barn.

The smile blooming across Grace's features only deepened as the buildings faded from sight behind them. She reined her mare down to a walk. "How long do you think before they'll notice?"

He settled Poncho into an easy stride beside Grace's mare. "Jacob promised to keep Anna busy. I think that's the only way we got out of there without a ruckus."

The ride to the river passed too quickly, as Monty soaked up time alone with this woman. His wife.

As the flowing water of the Guadalupe came into view, their conversation drifted into the peaceful sounds of nature. They reined in at a live oak tree, and Monty dismounted, then stepped around to help his bride.

Not that she needed help, but with her in that frilly blue dress he couldn't stand to keep his distance from her.

As he stepped near her mare, she gave him one of those looks that warmed his blood. He reached up to her waist and slipped her down to the ground. But now that he was this close, he wasn't letting go just yet.

She came into his arms willingly, and fit there like she'd been created for the spot. He held her close, breathing in the scent of summer roses in her hair. The trickle of the river before them drifted on the breeze.

"The day's been perfect so far. I just wish I could bring you to our new home tonight."

She shifted in his arms to look at him. "I don't mind, Monty."

He sank into those blue depths. "You don't mind bedding down in the extra bunkhouse for a few weeks?"

The corners of her mouth tipped. "Anywhere with you is home."

And that's exactly the way he felt. As they stood on the banks of the Guadalupe River, his wife in his arms, he'd never felt so complete.

What God brought together here—would last forever.

Did you enjoy Monty and Grace's story? I hope so!
Would you take a quick minute to leave a review?
It doesn't have to be long. Just a sentence or two telling what you liked about the story!

To receive a FREE short story and get updates when new Misty M. Beller books release, click here: mistymbeller.com/freebook

And here's a peek at Book 1 in the Wyoming Mountain Tales series, *A Pony Express Romance*:

Chapter One

November 30, 1860
Ellwood, Kansas

"Don't move, or I'll shoot ya right through the ticker."

Josiah English froze as the hard metal of a rifle barrel pressed into his back. His horse danced beneath him, complaining against his stranglehold on the reins. He didn't dare release the pressure, though. Not until he had a better grasp on the situation. He tilted his chin ever so slowly, scanning the perimeter to get a look at his captor.

The click of a rifle's set trigger rang loud in his ears, and the air stilled around him.

"I said *freeze*."

The sharp bark drew him up. His blood galloped, pounding in his ears as anger started to build. He wasn't a coward to be so easily taken by this highway bandit. But was there more than one? He forced air in through his nose and out through his mouth as he strained to decipher the noises behind him.

A whizzing sound flew by his ears, and within the same heartbeat, a rope settled around his shoulders. He jerked to pull it off, but the line yanked tight, strapping his arms to his sides. With a violent lurch, he was snatched sideways from his horse. For a second, his right foot caught in the stirrup, stretching him between opposite forces like a deer hide ready for tanning. Pain shot through his midsection. Would they rip his leg off?

His foot finally slipped from the stirrup, and for a moment he was airborne. Then he landed hard on the ground, the thud ricocheting through his back as the rope clenched tight around his midsection. The air exploded from his lungs. His chest seized, fighting a weight that threatened to smother him as he struggled to breathe.

At last, a precious breath seeped in, and awareness filtered into Josiah's oxygen-starved brain. He lay on the grass, staring into the blue November sky. A shadow moved across his vision —the dark outline of a man.

Josiah squinted to make out features. A dirty face loomed over him, with bushy black brows and a cigar protruding from thin lips.

He fought against the binding around his arms and chest, but the press of cold, round steel in his right temple froze his struggle.

"Take off his boots," Bushy Brows growled around his cigar.

Another man moved to Josiah's feet, this one tall and skinny with a blond, handle-bar moustache and droopy eyes. He grasped the heel of Josiah's left boot and pulled, setting off alarm bells in Josiah's head. *Not the boots.*

He jerked his foot hard, then kicked out toward the man, but the robber's long fingers clung to the heel like a barnacle on a ship's hull. The gun barrel pressed harder against his temple, pushing his head sideways into the grass.

"Get his boot off."

Josiah paused his fighting, sucking in breaths to steady himself so he could put together a plan. He may not be stronger than the force of that rifle, but maybe he could catch them in a blunder and overpower them.

The skinny man gripped Josiah's shoe and pulled. He couldn't stop himself from flexing his foot to make it harder for the brute to remove the leather.

The man struggled for a moment, then grunted and landed a hard kick in Josiah's shin. Pain ripped through his leg, loosening the muscles in his foot. The scrawny man jerked again, pulling the black leather free.

Papers slipped out as he turned the boot upside down—an image of a rider on a running horse flashing across the top. Josiah released a breath. Only his dispatch papers for the Pony Express, not the more precious documents.

Then Mustache reached for his other boot. The muscles in Josiah's shoulders tightened again. But he was in no position to win a fight yet. He could push through the pain in his left shin, but the rope around his chest bound his arms to his sides, and the cold steel pressed against his head kept him immobile.

The other boot slid off and a stack of money fluttered to the ground. He could picture the bills without looking—tens and fifties issued by the Southern Bank of Georgia. Black and red print forming letters, numbers, and pictures.

Half of his life savings. Maybe they'd be happy with their loot and stop searching.

Mustache jumped on the bills as they landed in the grass, clutching them in his grubby paws. Then he turned the boot upside down and dumped the remaining papers.

"Woo-wee, Charlie. We got us a good'n this time." The man's mustache lifted to reveal teeth of varying shades of brown.

"Keep lookin'," Charlie barked.

The gun barrel dug harder into Josiah's skull. He hoped in spades the man's trigger finger wasn't eager for exercise.

Mustache moved his search upward to Josiah's belly, a sneer taking over his face when he felt the money pouch Josiah had tucked under his shirt. When the man jerked the tail out of his trousers, cold air blasted Josiah's abdomen, raising goose flesh across his skin. The wiry man pounced on the pockets sewn into the cloth band.

Right pocket first. A handful of one dollar bills and a paper listing the Express stops he was to follow. The man kept the cash and tossed the document aside.

Left pocket. Another thick roll of bills. Josiah's stomach roiled, bile churning with his breakfast. They were taking everything he had. Everything he'd worked day and night to save for the last twelve years. The money to start his own ranch. His future.

The man's ugly face wobbled in Josiah's vision. The edges of his sight grew blurry as anger pulsed through him.

Josiah strained to focus on their actions. They rolled him onto his stomach and sweat pasted his shirt to his skin. The rifle barrel moved to his back.

After finding nothing when they patted him down a final time, Mustache seemed to be done with the search. The men exchanged words, their voices coming through Josiah's foggy brain like the buzzing of a bee. He struggled to make his mind focus again.

The gun came away from his back, and the ground thudded with the sound of boots tromping away from him. He twisted around—pulling against the rope biting into his arms—just in time to see the two men tearing down the road on horseback. They were headed west, the same direction he'd been traveling. Were those the kind of men he could expect to encounter in this new territory? He'd have to strengthen his defenses. The pistol tucked in his saddle pack had done little to help him with this fiasco.

He struggled to sit, then exhaled a long breath. With his hands, he loosened the lasso enough to slip it off over his head. At least they hadn't tied his hands and feet. Speaking of his feet, he glanced down at them, his wool socks left exposed without his boots. He reached into his left sock and pulled the small wad of ten dollar bills out from under the arch of his foot.

Fifty dollars. All that was left of his hard work and scrimping. It would get him to his destination at the Rocky Ridge Pony Express station, but wouldn't be enough to buy land, build a house and barn, and purchase good Arabian breeding stock. He wrapped his arms around his knees, dropped his head to his wrists, and took deep breaths.

Inhale. Exhale.

At least he had a job. A good one at that. He'd earn a hundred dollars a month riding for the Express—and improve his horse skills in the process. Now he'd have to stay on longer than the six months he'd planned. But he would still get his ranch, even if he had to scrape and save another few years. He wouldn't be stopped this easily.

Josiah raised his head and looked around. They hadn't even left his boots. The only things still lying in the grass were his papers from the Express.

He took another long breath, then exhaled. His horse had disappeared, and he was shoeless. At least he was alive with nothing broken. He pushed up to his feet, then strode to the road and considered both ways. If he went left, it was about two miles back to Ellwood. In the other direction, roughly seven miles on to Troy. It'd be quicker to go back the way he came and get a fresh horse. Start over.

Josiah sighed, then headed left. One painful step in front of the other on the rocky lane.

Around the first bend in the road, his bay gelding munched a patch of clover. The lean, muscled animal ate as if it hadn't seen green grass in a month of Tuesdays. At least someone was pleased with this situation.

Josiah eased forward, and the horse's ears flicked, but it never stopped ripping at the clover stems. He released a sigh as his hand closed around one of the reins. Stroking the gelding, he checked his saddle bags. Good. His Colt revolver and the few personal possessions were still secure. He lifted a stockinged foot into the stirrup and swung up.

The sun arced a couple hours short of high noon, and he'd been ordered to report at the Rocky Ridge stop on the Sweetwater River by December sixth, just six days from now. He didn't have time to stop for lunch, much less go back to Ellwood to report the bandits. He'd do it at the next town.

Lord, please let them have boots for sale there.

SWEETWATER RIVER VALLEY, WYOMING TERRITORY

Only a few more miles.

Josiah pushed his horse to a canter. This animal's rocking-horse rhythm was much smoother than the last two mounts he'd had. Changing horses every day had been interesting. Even though he wasn't on an official mail ride, the man at the Pony Express office in St. Joseph said he should ride Express-owned horses and stay at the regular stations—anything to get him to Rocky Ridge faster. He'd be taking over the mail line from a man who'd been injured, so the riders on the neighboring lines were pulling double duty until he could get there.

And after six days on the road, the boulder-strewn hills and buttes he'd been maneuvering now leveled into a rocky grassland. Should only have a couple miles left to the station he would call home.

Already, he felt like an Express rider. That is, now that every move didn't make his body scream. Riding horses woke up parts of his insides he hadn't known existed. But after living in the saddle this last week, his muscles were getting used to the new life.

He'd passed a couple of other Express riders along the way, mostly at the stations. It made his blood pump to see one of them tear out with the mail bag on a fresh horse, as if a pack of Indians was on his tail.

Indians… Josiah scanned the tree line on his left again. No visible movement. At the last few stations where he'd slept, the men shared quite a few stories about Paiute braves attacking Express riders, or burning down stations and stealing the horses. Josiah touched the wooden grip protruding from his waistband. His Colt revolver waited ready, should the need arise.

He turned his attention back to the horizon in front of him where the gray-blue sky merged into pinks and purples. In the fading light, a cluster of buildings stood in the middle of the flat, grassy stretch. A niggle of anxiety tugged in Josiah's chest. This would be his home station for a while. Would he like the people here? It didn't matter. He'd learned to live with whatever was necessary to accomplish what he'd set out for. Life wasn't an easy walk down a country lane. Not for a single moment.

He pulled his horse back to a jog, then reined her to a walk for the last few minutes. The bay mare was lathered, but her breathing returned to normal by the time they rode into the little courtyard between the four buildings. The structure on his left stood the largest by far, and looked to be the barn.

Josiah kicked his feet from the stirrups and rotated his ankles. Sharp needles pierced all the way up his calves, so he let his feet dangle for a moment until the pain lessened.

The door opened in the cabin to his right. On the threshold, a woman paused, then strode down the step and toward him. Her blue dress swished around her feet as she walked, determination marking her stride. She was a willowy thing, and wore her brown hair tied back in a way that revealed the strong curve of her jaw and the slope of her neck. Pretty, but younger than he'd expect for the stationmaster's wife. And she didn't look hardened enough to have lived long in this uncivilized country. Maybe she was passing through on one of the stagecoaches that followed this route.

She neared, close enough to rest a hand on the bay's neck, then brought up the other to shield her eyes from the sun as she looked at him. Those eyes. Even with the shadow of her hand, their shiny brown was wide enough for him to see clear through to her soul. The other features on her face were strong and balanced, maybe even refined, but those eyes pulled his focus so he had to fight to look away.

Pull yourself together, English. Josiah reined in his thoughts and removed his hat.

"Hello." Her voice was sweet and soft. "You're the new Express rider?" He strained to catch her words.

He nodded. And several seconds passed before he realized she waited for him to speak. "Yes, ma'am." He cleared his throat to steady the pitch of his voice. He was ogling like one of the simple-minded wharf-workers where he'd grown up in Savannah.

She didn't seem to notice his clumsiness—or at least, had the grace to ignore it. Instead, she reached for the mare's reins and pulled the loop over the horse's head. "Go on and get settled in the bunkhouse." She nodded toward the shed-like building next to the barn. "I'll get this girl taken care of, then finish dinner. When I ring the bell, come to the main house to eat." She pointed a thumb toward the structure behind her.

He swallowed to work some moisture into his mouth. She must belong to the place. "Is your...uh...husband around?"

Her lips pinched, and one corner quirked up. Her big brown

gaze met his, light dancing there. "No husband. But my brothers are in the barn haying the horses."

The tension in his chest eased, but he tried not to look too deep into the reason. It sounded like she had men here to protect her. But not a husband.

Sliding from the horse, Josiah caught himself so he landed softly on his sore ankles. "I'll get my saddle bags before you take her." His fingers fumbled with the leather straps. Finally, he had both the front and back bags off, and she led the horse away without another word.

Even the weariness in his bones didn't stop him from watching her go, her long skirt feathering across the tops of the grass as she stepped with a self-assured grace.

His mouth pressed in a frown. Why hadn't he asked her name?

Get A PONY EXPRESS ROMANCE at your favorite retailer.

ABOUT THE AUTHOR

Misty M. Beller is a *USA Today* bestselling author of romantic mountain stories, set on the 1800s frontier and woven with the truth of God's love.

She was raised on a farm in South Carolina, so her Southern roots run deep. Growing up, her family was close, and they continue to keep that priority today. Her husband and children now add another dimension to her life, keeping her both grounded and crazy.

God has placed a desire in Misty's heart to combine her love for Christian fiction and the simpler ranch life, writing historical novels that display God's abundant love through the twists and turns in the lives of her characters.

Connect with Misty at www.MistyMBeller.com

ALSO BY MISTY M. BELLER

Call of the Rockies

Freedom in the Mountain Wind

Hope in the Mountain River

Light in the Mountain Sky

Courage in the Mountain Wilderness

Faith in the Mountain Valley

Honor in the Mountain Refuge

Brides of Laurent

A Warrior's Heart

Hearts of Montana

Hope's Highest Mountain

Love's Mountain Quest

Faith's Mountain Home

Texas Rancher Trilogy

The Rancher Takes a Cook

The Ranger Takes a Bride

The Rancher Takes a Cowgirl

Wyoming Mountain Tales

A Pony Express Romance

A Rocky Mountain Romance

A Sweetwater River Romance

A Mountain Christmas Romance

The Mountain Series

The Lady and the Mountain Man

The Lady and the Mountain Doctor

The Lady and the Mountain Fire

The Lady and the Mountain Promise

The Lady and the Mountain Call

This Treacherous Journey

This Wilderness Journey

This Freedom Journey (novella)

This Courageous Journey

This Homeward Journey

This Daring Journey

This Healing Journey

Made in the USA
Middletown, DE
08 August 2023